IN A SECRET PLACE

BOOKS BY JOHN WOOD

In a Secret Place

Trouble at Mrs Portwine's

Charlie and the Stinking Ragbags

W.H.I.F.F.

In a
Secret Place

John Wood

WOLFHOUND PRESS

Paperback 1993
© 1993, 1986 John Wood

First published in hardback in 1986 by
WOLFHOUND PRESS
68 Mountjoy Square, Dublin 1.

British Library Cataloguing in Publication Data

Wood, John
  In a Secret Place. – New ed
  I. Title
  823.914   [J]

  ISBN 0-86327-399-8 Pbk
  ISBN 0-86327-180-4 Hbk

Wolfhound Press receives financial assistance from
The Arts Council (An Chomhairle Ealaíon), Dublin, Ireland.

Cover illustration: Katharine White
Typesetting: Redsetter Ltd, Dublin
Printed by the Guernsey Press Co Ltd, Guernsey, Channel Isles

CONTENTS

To Tom and Gwyn Turner
of Drumcondra in Dublin

PART ONE

1

Gifts of Food

AFTER THE CEREMONY, the bride's gypsy family stood on the chapel steps with eyes half closed against the winter sunlight. The unfamiliar church smells, the pink organ pipes and what the preacher had said; all of it making them feel awkward.

Wilfred found himself listening intently to the pigeons calling from the nearby trees, unaware of the photographer's voice, with a sharp edge to it, as he said "Smile *please!*"

Again, a pigeon, its eye flinty with watching, had called into this strange well of silence, in which it seemed they had gathered for a moment in their lives.

In certain moods Wilfred would hear or see countryside things very clearly and it would send shudders into his thin body. Instead of a feeling of anger with the rain coming into his clothes or with nettle stings, he would see temples in the hedges: shrines of rosy red twigs and brown twigs: berries of all colours. He felt delirious with joy now: deeply aware of the wild beauty of the winter about him.

His bride was next to him.

He had kept a photograph of course: looking in that nervous way; squinting because of the sunlight in their eyes. There had been that unfamiliar smell of perfume of the bride and he had felt so proud to be near her like this: not being asked to move away. If he had been a man of old he would have offered a sheep in slaughter, in the joy he felt about it, although he happened not to like killing.

Her hand had nestled in his like a mole: a wild animal he had taken into safety from the hedgelands and the woods.

Wilfred had been gathering primroses from a slope by the edge of a wood. These he would sell to the people in the new houses. Sometimes he was offered a packet of tea instead. Most of the time he made clothes pegs; cutting strips of tin from old cans, which he nailed around the top of the peg. First he washed out the cans in the brook. He was not quick at making the posies. He had watched the gypsy girls do it. Now he straightened his back and sighed at the thought of making pegs again.

A voice had called out: "A child could do better!"

He had looked up. She was standing at the top of the bank. Although he cupped his hands to his eyes he could see only her outline. Her hair was a blaze of silver as she blotted out the sun.

She laughed, "What a mess. My sister and she's not ten could do it better!"

"Show me," Wilfred said.

"I will at that!" She slid down the bank. Going straight to the flowers: squatting down and moving from one clump to another, still crouched down.

"Look!" she said when she had finished, "Look."

But Wilfred had looked only at her face now turned towards him. He had seen clearly: on the cool slope under the willow tree, her brown hair, and her lips as red as the red berries.

That was how they had met.

The field above the primrose bank had been built upon. The rough old willow had been wrenched out of the black ground: the same tree under which Wilfred, standing there had seen her for the first time.

Now his chin and neck around to his ears was covered with a mostly white beard. There was some grey in it and some sparkling colours.

He had stayed on in the town, living in a single room. He would often walk into the surrounding countryside; cutting willow and looking into hedges for old kettles. These he would take to E. Mabbs & Son, the scrap-iron man who owned the room in which he lived.

When it was spring, he avoided places where primroses grew.

Although not a gypsy like his wife, he had been a travelling man. Often he walked the town roads near his room, with a travelling feeling.

In the spring he would cut people's hedges.

Then he cut the willow for his clothes pegs, after the primroses had died down.

She had left home.

Thinner than ever, Wilfred walked the hilly streets, in his light uncertain way; stopping sometimes in doorways; pulling out his flute; smiling at people. They would nod and walk on.

But the wife of the preacher had spoken to him. He had been unable to stop talking. Her face was altering as the words poured out. She kept on smiling with her eyes still serious; then looking down; raising her arms helplessly.

Seeing the preacher's wife had made Wilfred talk of the days that were gone for ever. "And she tells me, every time, whenever, whatever it is," he said nonsensically, slowing down, beginning to shiver. "Cleaning the pots or whatever. 'My sister could do better.' Then when her sister is a grown woman. 'There is a child next door: up the street.' It doesn't matter where. 'This child' she tells me, 'could do it better.'"

All the preacher's wife had said, touching his arm: not with her flat hand but with her fingers, arching, as if she was testing the top of a hot stove, was:

"You're looking after your daughter all alone, I hear. I will send you some veal and ham pie. I will send it in the morning."

Then he had spoken like that, so that she was weak with relief when he left. Perhaps it was this that put the pie out of her mind for two weeks or more.

*   *   *

So he would go down the High Street.

He knew people did not want to talk. To make matters worse, if passers-by smiled, he would bring out his flute. Then he would go from shop to shop: standing for a long time looking at the waxy apples or the shoes or anything else.

Someone gave him a hat and he would take it from his head in the old fashioned way, in a silent greeting.

Alice knew why people kept away from her father. It was because of his extraordinariness. Sometimes she would go with him on his long walks: watching the sky and the wild flowers: listening to Wilfred explain things about the countryside that ordinary people did not understand. In the hot weather, putting her toes in the brook while Wilfred played his flute; gazing at the far-away woods and the fields of different greens.

Children she knew had said she and Wilfred were gypsy people. She knew this was not strictly true, although perhaps her mother had been. It was only in the town that there was a feeling of shame. She wished there could be more ordinariness in the way they were.

Alice did not recognize it as shame. It was not the way she felt all the time. Certainly not when she was in the countryside. Once, when Wilfred was cutting garden hedges, she had waited for him on the pavement outside, looking at a brass pot in the window, and a cat.

A lady said "Is that your father?"

"No," said Alice.

"My cat is called Mendip."

"No! No! No!" Alice said again, biting her teeth together hard: a flush staining her cheeks; even her lips going dark red. It happened like this always, when she became close to tears. The reason for this sudden shame that overwhelmed and hurt was Wilfred's boots. She did not know why he had lately taken to doing it. When he played his flute, it would look noticeable as he tapped his foot.

He had painted his boots silver.

The butcher would strike his chopper into the bones speaking gently to the mother or the widow smelling of lavender water; wrapping the meat up with flourishes, making papery noises, as if he was an actor. Saying things like "There my love. Don't forget the carrots." Then "Next one please. What do you want, sonny?" His voice changing.

He was being the butcher and people understood this.

Wilfred often kept in the far-away places of the town, not making a nuisance of himself. Sitting in quiet shop places, off the pavement; where there might be flaky paint on the window frames and beetles in the skirting. There would be a worried looking shop keeper in the glassy shadows, peering into the street.

People could not understand Wilfred's sort of extraordinariness.

No one except Alice knew about Wilfred.

He was not anybody in particular.

Sometimes Alice thought: How could they know about what the brook was like in flood: the same brook that cooled her feet in the hot summer days? Of long winter roads and brown hedges looking for lost kettles? Alice had seen woodsap running from a cut tree. Some of them had never seen woodsap!

Wilfred had seen ravens sitting on a post; noticed the ruffled back feathers shining and black; blown in a soft wind, which ever so gently carried the smells of popped seeds.

All of this sort of thing, when other people would be turning sausages or trying on a dress in the inside of a building.

So Wilfred was different and did things like painting his boots. Or playing his flute; his thin fingers moving swiftly over it, his body trembling as he thought of the primroses and her voice saying softly, "My sister could do it better." Well show me. Show me, show me.

It was a summer's day. There were no persistent thoughts gathering like shadows on a hill; nor memories like this, making Wilfred silent.

He was striding down the main street. His eyes blue like the sky; with no clouds to be seen. The sun shone on the motor cars and the carts; the red and yellow colours of them as fleshy looking as the hedge berries. Going into the butcher shop for soup bones he said "Good morning!" Then "Good morning!"

again. He was smiling: restless. His flute was in his pocket and he gripped it; held from playing it by the butcher's eye.

Then he went into the street. To strangers he said "Good morning!" raising his hat high into the sparrowy air. Out of the corner of their eyes, people saw him; his silver boots bright in the sunlight; moving so lightly and curiously down the street that he could have been dancing. The preacher's wife saw him straggling towards her from the apple shop and she turned away. He had been sent the veal and ham pie.

Others too were now sending him a little food. Sometimes, out on a walk, he would look guiltily at the old thrown away cans that he used to clean and cut into strips; and at the young willow trees. Because of the food he was being given he had less reason for making pegs. Also people gave him money, although he had not intended it to happen. When there were no gifts of food, he begged for it.

*   *   *

Today he had stepped up the hill, away from the preacher's wife, the cars, the carts and the tailor's shop. Trees shaded the big houses. An elderly man with a silver pencil in his top pocket said "How d'you do" uncertainly, his white eyebrows quivering as he tried to focus on Wilfred. When he saw the boots and his straggling beard lit up by the speckled light, he quickened his pace away from him.

Wilfred was tempted to bring his flute out. But the respectability of the neighbourhood overwhelmed him. Now he stood unseen, by a window at the back of the Mayor's kitchen. A fan was drawing out the cooking smells. Wilfred breathed deeply, closing his eyes. Ah, he thought, that is pork. Perhaps with apple sauce. Coffee to be sure! His nose quivered. The door opened. The cook said: "Here, take this. Go away now." Wilfred said nothing. He took the bag with the food. Pork, he was right!

For an instant it seemed that Wilfred was about to break into a dance. "Don't you dare!" said the cook, looking at the flute. "Off you go!" He put the bag in his pocket with the flute. He returned to his home by the back streets, although at one stage he passed the town hall, pausing as he did so to lift his hat to do it, saying, "Your Honour won't miss a little meat now will you?"

But Alice said, "Why do it? My friends know you ask for things." Wilfred did not answer; sitting himself in his armchair.

"We will have a little meat for tea," he said. "Would you like a little meat?"

"I have got some beans on toast all ready for us."

"Add a little meat to it!"

"I don't want any. You can eat it all yourself." Alice went to the window, which overlooked Mabbs' scrap iron yard, her shoulders pushed forward; trying not to answer.

"You're tired," Wilfred said. "You should not wait up for owls, like you have been doing."

"I must listen for owls," Alice said.

"People your age should be fast asleep when the owls are about."

"But I must listen," Alice said softly, her shoulders relaxing.

"Well maybe, for your own reasons," said Wilfred, "in the same way with little habits that is, I like visiting the kitchens of the rich people." Adding: "I doubt anyway if they know me."

Alice turned, as if to question him.

"I come back a crooked way," explained Wilfred, "all the time."

2

Practising Owls

THE FAN IN THE MAYOR'S KITCHEN had been switched off. Beads of water collected on the glass; running down; distorting the faces of the cook, the butler and the maid. They were seated at the kitchen table, laughing and talking.

Then a bell rang. The last beads of water broke free and the pane was clear. Showing the butler's face, which had become still at the instant. The maid said: "Old Horrible wants you. You'd better go then." She pushed away her coffee cup as if she had suddenly lost interest in it, and stared at the bell high up on the wall. It rang once for her, twice for the cook and three times for the butler.

The Mayor had cunning black eyes and a moon-coloured face; a jungle-coloured moon: the kind that shines on the backs of drowsing rhinoceroses. He ran his hand over his silk waistcoat.

"Tell Cook the apple sauce was too sour."

"Yes Sir."

"My son," said the Mayor, "is not at table."

"Paul, Sir?"

"I have no other son, although very often I wish . . ." He turned to his wife. "Pass me the nuts my dear."

Then to the butler he said: "Why have you not seen to it that Paul was at table? Have you looked in the pigeon loft?"

"He was not there, Sir. But early on I did hear him I think. That is . . ."

"Come along!"

"He was practising owls."

"You may go," said the Mayor.

His wife's heavy eyelids were nearly closed. The Mayor believed this to be brought about by concentration, which pleased him. In fact she had a narrow misty sight of him like this; seeing only a small amount of him. She could safely dream the dreams of childhood: lying in the grass, watching the dragonflies; opening the pickled onion jar.

Sometimes he would say: "What do you think of that?"

Struggling to remember, keeping her lids shut, she would say: "You must give me time to consider it."

But now, quite clearly he had said: "And I tell you something else about our son!"

His hands were fluttering over the nut dish. He dusted his waistcoat, then ran his fingers slowly down his cheek.

"There is" he said, now rubbing his cheek very hard, "no marzipan left in the cupboard. He likes marzipan. I have seen his face when he is eating it."

"A little something," she said weakly.

"Exactly so. But it has all gone!"

Again, he rang for the butler. Pulling the bell rope; grasping the important looking velvet tassle; clenching it very hard so that for a moment his white girl's skin was flushed bright red about the ring on his finger.

"Now, Sir," said the Mayor, "tell me, if you will."

"Yes, Sir," said the butler nervously.

His wife had firmly closed her eyes again.

"I'm glad of it," the Mayor said. He had risen from the table and paced up and down as he spoke. "You said he was practising owls?"

"Sir."

"How? Well come on, show us! Hoot away, Sir." To his wife he said "Pass the nuts, my dear."

But the servant's lips had dried on his teeth and he could not make a sound.

"You may go," said the Mayor after a while.

He stared at Paul's untouched plate. His face was whiter than ever, with an ordinary sort of moon colour, and his eyes moved restlessly like snakes, as he thought of the way his son had insulted him.

*   *   *

Adjoining Mr Mabbs' scrap iron yard was a marshy field. His old white horse was tethered on the higher slopes where it was dry. In the winter people kept to the trodden paths: coughing, shivering in the cold mist; keeping away from the black mud and the reeds.

Once, the horse had broken its tether; galloping wildly over the field in terror; its eye as bright and hard as the ice itself; frightened by a metal bucket which had been dashed over the frozen field by the wind.

Alice often looked out of their top-floor window at Mr Mabbs' scrapyard and the field. Now it was streaked with green; spiky with summer flowers: buttercup, clover and vetch. Through the buttercup places ran a brook. As Alice looked, she felt her lip going stiff and peculiar, as it did when she was excited. A boy's head bobbed up from the tall grasses that grew by the banks of the brook. He was looking at his watch. Then he brought out a knife from his pocket. He re-shaped the prow of the boat he had made and again tried sitting it on the water, this time with success.

The boy gazed for a long time at the brook. As if gathering himself from a dream, he suddenly yelled. Now he was running, leaping across the brook with such force that he rolled over and over in the buttercups. He did this several times before tiring of it.

Mabbs' horse looked up, then shook its head because of the flies and went on eating.

Alice turned away.

3

Yanina and the Lavender Scent

THE BROOK TRICKLED through the field towards the town. Beyond the field, the brook divided the gardens of the houses on either side of it. It was barely a foot wide, with steep sides. In some places more than others it smelled of wet earth and wild watercress, especially where it had been trodden down.

The afternoon sun moved to the dresser with the brightly coloured cups. The back door was open and Yanina stood still where she was, in the kitchen listening to her aunt with Mr Potter. On the waxy table were two plates and in the centre, on a lace mat, an untouched cherry cake. It was not tea time, but her aunt always liked to have everything prepared in advance.

"If I was in Mrs Potter's position needing the money as no doubt you do, I would have bandaged my ankle up."

"She has," said Mr Potter.

"And come to work," she said, ignoring him.

As he went by the kitchen window, Yanina whistled softly through the gap in her front teeth.

"Is Mrs Potter bad?" she whispered.

He was about to answer, his features softening, but suddenly he seemed to think better of it.

"Yanina," said her aunt, her head beginning to nod with agitation, "come with me. Mrs Potter cannot do the house-work because she is ill, poor thing."

They stood in the dim hallway. On the first landing was a large window: some of it stain-glassed. One was of a coat of arms which was like the colour of forgotten mustard. In the corners the light glinted through four blue flowers. The banister shone with wax. Her aunt stood by the stairs, her head nodding rhythmically. "And as she is not well, you can polish the staircase yourself. You are well I hope, dear?"

Yanina polished up to the first landing and then to the second landing. The mellowing sunlight cast a patch of blue on the window cill from one of the flowers in the glass. She worked steadily, stopping only once to put her finger in the blue light. A clock chimed and presently her aunt called.

"You may come to tea Yanina!"

The brook! It was time! She looked out of the window at their back garden sloping down towards it. "I am coming," she called.

"Aunt," she said, "I feel peculiar. May I go outside?"

"Have you done all the polishing?"

"Yes."

"You look very well to me," her aunt said. Very well indeed with her black eyes and milky skin! She rubbed her finger in the soft hair on her upper lip.

"I need some air," Yanina said.

"Tea will not wait," her aunt replied.

"But I must go down to the brook," she said in a surprising way.

There in the corner of the kitchen were the sunlit cups and Uncle Stephen's telescope.

A linnet sang from a bush. Yanina was aware of all these things as she gazed at her aunt. It gave her a feeling of not being afraid.

"I will feel better soon," she said going to the door. Out of the corner of her eye she saw her aunt cut into the cherry cake. A piece of it fell from her hand on to the table.

Mr Carey was bending down picking strawberries. They were end to end neighbours in the sense that his back garden also finished at the brook. Occasionally now he whistled half tunes. He straightened his back and sighed. He had not seen Yanina. She sat on the bank, hidden by the tall grasses.

Mr Carey and Mr and Mrs Potter were her friends: Mr Carey especially. He was old and his trousers were of unusually coarse cloth. Yesterday his fingers had been red because of the strawberries. She expected it would be the same today. Mr Carey had said it was because they were too ripe but Yanina thought it was because his fingers groped so clumsily into the strawberry plants. His eyesight was poor. Sometimes she could see his face between his legs as he bent down.

She was wondering if it would be rude to say 'good afternoon' in that way of seeing each other. Then she turned round sharply but there was no one there. She looked back at the house, feeling a tightening of the skin on the top of her head.

The water flowed noisily over some thrown away bricks.

The boat was passing the buttercups that grew on the bank; the brook darkened with their green and yellow mantle; half submerged stones stank as they dried in the sun. The boat was going towards the whiskery Mr Carey. He had filled two boxes made of thin woven wood, almost as thin as wood shavings.

The smells and summery sounds made Yanina feel quite dozy and she called out suddenly, without wondering whether or not it would be polite, "Good afternoon Mr Carey!"

The boat had lodged against a twig. Then a water rat swam by, its brown eyes unwinking. It looked at the land and the shapes on it. Now the boat was free and came unhindered to where Yanina was. She took it: lifting it up. The prow dripped water on to her skirt. It was not as long as her hand. The sail was of paper. She tore this off and read the message on it. Then she threw the boat back on the water. The weight of the mast keeping it on its side.

Standing up, she put the message in her blouse pocket. In her excitement her foot had slipped on the wet bank and a great cloud of gnats rose up, circling round and round.

Her socks were spattered with mud.

"Oh dear," said Yanina, "she won't like that. Not a bit!"

The boat stayed on its side all the way to where the brook joined the river, which was almost as wide as Mabbs' field. Where the river flowed under the town bridge the boat was sucked down into its brown water.

* * *

The cake had been taken away. Yanina helped herself to a slice of bread that had been put in its place, watched carefully by her aunt as she did so.

She was determined to show no signs of disappointment. But as her aunt left the table to answer the door, she grimaced, pushing her tongue between her front teeth.

"So you're here!" her aunt was saying.

"Yes ma'am." It was Mrs Potter. "I bandaged it like you said to Mr Potter."

"It's too bad for you! The work is done."

"I am sorry ma'am," Mrs Potter said. "It happened . . ."

Yanina half listened to the voices, staring dreamily at the dresser with the cups and the odds and ends. In particular she was thinking about Uncle Stephen's telescope.

No one knew exactly what had become of Uncle Stephen, except that the crew had taken to the boats. His empty ship had been found drifting in the lazy sea, after a storm. Yanina remembered him in the far distance. Sometimes he had told her about the ship and particularly of his desk; the ship's diary and quill pen; and of the way the ship shook and trembled in the huge green seas. They had found the pen and the diary and brass telescope on his desk and the menu for the next day. 'Cream of Asparagus Soup' had been crossed out and in its place Uncle Stephen had written 'French Onion Soup'.

The interesting thing about the telescope at the moment was that it had been moved! It was not looking like that when she had gone to the brook.

The voices had ceased. Had her aunt watched her with it? Perhaps seen her put the message in her blouse! Yanina ran to the stove. She thrust the message into the flames, replacing the lid noiselessly. She stood with her back to the stove, shivering, as her aunt came in.

"What is the matter with you?" said her aunt impatiently. The shivering had become worse, particularly in her stomach.

"Take off your blouse for the wash. Give it to me!"

Mechanically Yanina undid the buttons. Well she would find nothing!

"Now upstairs to bed."

She knew her aunt would already be searching her blouse. Walking up the stairs past the stained-glass window she said to herself again and again: She will find nothing! there is nothing! Yanina did not touch the oak banisters, not wanting to feel the wax. Her room was high up in the attic. Mr Carey had gone indoors. In places the brook gleamed and in the distance Mr Mabbs' horse stood white and pearly in the last shreds of daylight.

She did not mind going to bed early. Part of the message was 'Have a good night's sleep'. But she stayed awake for a long time, tossing and turning, looking at the wooden ceiling with the dark brown knots. Some of them had fallen out. The room always smelled of the pineboard, especially in summer. In winter she could also smell it, even when the steam from a cup of cocoa came up into her face.

It also said that they could each take one thing with them, as long as it could be carried. One thing! She imagined all sorts of things. Sometimes she was half asleep and thinking of the objects became difficult, because she would slide off into dreams about them.

She would have liked to have taken Uncle Stephen's telescope. It would have been most useful. Looking close up at the violet coloured shadows and green hills and animals cleaning their fur; all of it moving very fast this way and that because of the difficulty of keeping the telescope still.

But she dared not take it.

One thing only! One thing!

Yanina had woken up suddenly in the dark, without knowing she had gone to sleep. She knew at that moment what she would take and quickly slept again, her mind at peace. It was a bottle of lavender scent Mr Carey had given her last Christmas. It was unopened. She had not opened it because of wanting to keep it, as it was, for a long time.

4

Don't Disturb Your Father

NAILED TO AN APPLE TREE in Mr Weekes' small front garden was a noticeboard on which was painted: 'George Weekes . . . tables. Enquiries Invited'. Pots of pink and red geraniums showed in every window of the ramshackle old building. There was little evidence of any other Weekes, except of course Mrs Weekes who seemed to be there so as to cook for, mend for and make tea for Mr Weekes.

Benjamin Weekes was not often seen. He spent much of his time in the pigeon loft, high up overlooking the neighbours' backyards. His ears stuck out. Sometimes he wished he could stand alone in the hot flowery jungle like an elephant with his large ears and be alone and uncaring; looking at the wild orchids growing in the trees. He also had hand warts. He was good at marbles and conkers. Sometimes he flushed deeply when spoken to.

Mr Weekes worked in the cellar. The afternoon sun shone through the ground level windows which were high up near the ceiling. There were rows of planes and chisels neatly displayed on shelves, saws, spoke shaves and all manner of tools, glue pots, stain pots and quantities of wood stacked all around the walls. In the centre was Mr Weekes' workbench adrift in a mass of wood shavings and tables in various stages of manufacture. Mr Weekes worked at speed, only pausing to look at what he had done. He would hum a tune: his thumb and finger rubbing his moustache hairs gently, as an expression of the intense satisfaction his work gave him.

Mrs Weekes took cups of tea to him. Benjamin, when he could be found carried the biscuit tin. Sometimes Benjamin would ask "What is that for?" or "What are you doing?" Mrs Weekes would always interrupt saying "Don't disturb your father."

The truth was that 'Enquiries were Not Invited' for his tables anymore. He was the supplier to the local store, telling people he had been appointed, in the way that jam makers and so on are appointed to make jam and other things for the Royal Family.

The shop was Goodbody, Arbuthnott and Wallis. Mr Wallis was the only one left. When customers came in he would walk over to them, his hands clasped in greeting; his bones cracking in his anxiety to please. 'Bony Wallis' as he was called, encouraged Mr Weekes, heaping praise upon him, so that he would not tire of making tables. "Ah Mr Weekes," he would say, "what legs! What a creation!"

Mr Weekes bought a floppy velvet hat, such as artists wear. In the warm evenings he would parade up and down the street with Mrs Weekes. Sometimes Benjamin might loiter behind them: looking up; seeing them in the distance as he played marbles on the pavement.

On Sunday afternoons Mr Weekes would sit in the chair by the fireplace, his short legs stuck out straight. Mrs Weekes gently wheeled about him tidying away the remains of the Sunday roast lunch; going over the furniture with the duster made of cockerel feathers. When he was asleep she would settle in the chair opposite him and take up her knitting.

On Sunday afternoons Benjamin was allowed in the cellar workshop: all nicely swept the day before by Mrs Weekes. The afternoon sun would pour its light on the huge floor and there Benjamin would practise marbles, sometimes stopping to watch the winking colours. He liked the smell of stain and woodshavings in sacks, ready for the bonfire on Monday. He did not go to the pigeon loft on Sundays, preferring the cellar. If after Sunday lunch he started to speak, his mother would say, "Don't disturb your father."

Benjamin had a bag of tools. It had been given to him by an uncle. When this relative came to the house, Mr Weekes would become agitated, making an unnecessary cut with his chisel or something like that. This uncle never forgot Benjamin's birthday. If the present was a shirt, his mother would run her fingers through it, saying "Much too rough" and send it to the second-hand shop next to the ironmongers. If it was a book she would take it away saying "What will he think of next?"

The bag of tools was put in a cupboard in the cellar workshop. They were fine woodworking tools. His mother could not bring herself to get rid of them, saying only "Perhaps when you are older," although she thought to herself that Mr Weekes would not like it even then.

Often Benjamin climbed up the step ladder to look at them, when the house was quiet and still on Sundays. He did not have the courage to ask his father how to use them, although when he went to the cellar with his mother he often stood there, holding the biscuit tin, watching him carefully, making certain not to speak. Sure enough if he did his mother would say "Don't disturb your father". After a while, in between playing marbles, he practised on bits of wood. He would make sure to replace the tools as they were. He put the shavings in the sacks.

One Sunday his parents had gone visiting. Mr Weekes wore his velvet hat.

"Your father has been working very hard on a special table," she said. "A bit of a creation really; and he needs an outing."

Instead of lunch Mrs Weekes left a whole ginger cake on the kitchen table together with a bottle of lemonade.

"We are expecting Mr Wallis, *the* Mr Wallis of Goodbody, Arbuthnott and Wallis, sometime after tea," she had said, adding "and we'll be back in good time don't you worry. But no mess!"

"You must tell the boy not to take the dust cloth off the table. It must be kept perfect for Mr Wallis," Mr Weekes said.

"You must not even peep at your father's new creation. Do you understand?"

Benjamin sat in his father's chair, eating cake and drinking lemonade. He whistled as he went to the cellar. He quickly tired of marbles and climbed up the steps for his tools. He did not even bother to look at his father's new table.

He practised.

Then he did something he had never done before. He started to make something.

Time played tricks. He only realized it was afternoon because of the sunlight coming through the windows, flooding the clean workshop floor. In the centre stood a small table. It was immensely simple and of great beauty. It would have looked right with wise men seated at it. Benjamin was thinking that kind jungly sort of animals would have looked most suitable as well. Then he whistled very loud and walked swiftly to it with a handful of glass marbles, thrusting them in the middle of the table.

The sunlight flashed in them with green fire and red and blue.

"Hello!" a voice called. "Is anyone there?"

Frantically Benjamin searched for a hammer to knock his table to bits: to hide it, to stuff it in the sacks . . . anything! But the door was opening, and he could not do it. So he kept silent. The thumping stopped in his head. Mr Wallis did not talk to him, although he must have seen Benjamin standing pressed against the wall.

Mr Wallis put his hands together and started cracking his finger bones furiously. He walked around the table and looked at it from different angles. Then he took out his handkerchief and blew his nose.

Benjamin saw Mr Wallis to the door. All Mr Wallis had said was "I will speak to him tomorrow. Blessed if I won't," and that was more in the manner of talking to himself.

Later Benjamin was about to go downstairs when his mother returned and called: "Ben, clean up the cake crumbs at once."

Then he heard a commotion through the hallway. Mr Weekes was laughing, so much that he afterwards complained of stomach pains. "That for one thing," his mother had said, "is not a good thing for your father. We can do without you straining him like that."

They had not even asked Benjamin if Mr Wallis had called.

"Oh well," said Mr Weekes, "I daresay he'll be calling tomorrow instead." Then talking directly to Benjamin, still in a good humour at the sight of the table: "Have one of my biscuits!"

Benjamin gulped his tea. He started to cough and splutter as he struggled to conceal the sobs that kept welling up inside him. They thought he was only choking on a biscuit.

Mr Wallis had sent a message round: would it be all right for him to call at 11 sharp? Two cups and saucers: one of them for Mr Wallis, were placed ready on a tray. A little water was in the pot, to keep it warm before making the tea.

Mrs Weekes felt it, drumming her fingers on it.

"Now Benjamin, go up to the loft and clean the cages. That is probably Mr Wallis at the door now and I don't want you to disturb your father."

Benjamin's table had been broken up and put in the sacks with the shavings. In its place, in the centre of the floor was Mr Weekes' new creation. It was a heavy looking table: a suffering-from-indigestion table at which Mayors in satin waistcoats with buttery fingers could sit. The plum-jam coloured wood was deeply polished.

Benjamin felt that something was about to go wrong, so he lingered on the landing safely out of sight where the stairs turned. He knew which particular board to miss because of its creak.

First of all Mrs Weekes came up the cellar steps in what seemed to be a hurry. She shut the kitchen door and turned on the wireless.

Mr Weekes was talking in a raised up voice, steadily like a saw whirring, waiting to get into wood, the blade whipping through the air in an angry whine. The feeling of anger and destruction made Benjamin feel faint. He looked at the position of the creaking floorboard, although he would not have been heard above the noise.

They were in the hall.

"I will not have it!" shouted Mr Weekes. "I will not listen to it on any account."

Mr Wallis was grimly saying, "Well maybe you won't. But it's too fussy. Try to capture the beauty, the simplicity."

"From a child! You are out of your mind!" He was white faced. His floppy velvet hat which he had worn for the occasion had fallen over one eye.

Mr Wallis did not call again. He sent round several messages, asking when he could expect delivery of tables. He tactfully did not refer to the new model.

Mr Weekes had repainted the sign in the front garden, underlining 'enquiries invited'. He was taking his table to other shops in different towns. He had bought an old van for the purpose. It was a faded green and the paint had cracked in so many places and been pulled together again with so much polishing that the surface looked like cow leather. Often he came back late at night, down the lanes, past the inky black streets. He woke up later in the mornings because he was tired. He did not make so many tables, although they were all the ordinary kind which before he had sold to Goodbody, Arbuthnott and Wallis.

Benjamin was sure that sometimes he went off again the next day with the same tables, because he had been unable to sell them. Mrs Weekes said once, with a worried edge to her voice, "George you didn't eat your sandwiches!"

When Mr Weekes was in the workshop, Benjamin was no longer allowed to follow his mother in with the biscuit tin. He was not allowed in the workshop on Sundays, so practising with bits of wood ended. In any case the tools had been hidden, although Benjamin knew where they were. Mr Weekes had said: "Well Mother, for his own good, you'd best tell him, he can have the tools when he's a man."

It was once after Sunday dinner. Mr Weekes' eyes were closed as he rested in his chair.

Mrs Weekes nodded at Benjamin as if to say: well you heard what he said I've no doubt.

She went on dusting the furniture with the duster made of cockerel feathers. Benjamin, who was just about to sneeze because of it, left quietly to go to the pigeon loft.

5

The Pigeon Loft

THE FIELDS WERE YELLOW AND GREEN with wheat not yet ripened; the corn not soft and milky if pressed. Sometimes Benjamin walked along the lanes where animals and flowers had lived in the high earthy banks; out into the edges of the countryside. But most of the time now he stayed in the pigeon loft. He was waiting for the return of Mr Yates, his favourite pigeon, who was at present held in the pigeon loft of his friend the Mayor's son.

From where he was he could look down on the back yards and small gardens of his neighbours. He often saw the old lady next door. The loft jutted out so that Benjamin could look into a piece of her kitchen quite easily, while making it seem that he was cleaning the boxes. In this way a friendship had grown. The lady would smile and nod up at him. Once she had come to the front door with a pot of jam. But Mrs Weekes had said she was a dirty lady. Benjamin had looked in the kitchen cupboards but had never found it. She beat her mat on the small lawn, after sitting at the kitchen table, on which stood a teapot and cup. Lately Benjamin noticed that she would take longer and longer with her tea drinking, sitting quite still, as the blackbirds wheeled and fussed in the garden singing their afternoon songs.

The summer breeze sighed in the loft. Smells from bonfires stole up to him. Crickets chirped. Sometimes Benjamin could smell bacon-cooking smells from the kitchen of the old lady. It was known that she was very fond of bacon.

He kept his marbles on a window cill in the loft and the sun would make them flash again. A few days earlier he had thrown one of them carefully on to her lawn, hoping the lady would find it and know where it had come from.

Benjamin saw the old lady hanging up her washing. She was using the old fashioned willow peg with a band of tin nailed round the top to stop it splitting in half. It would almost certainly have been made by Wilfred.

She dropped some clothing and bent to pick it up. Then she stopped again and picked up the marble, rubbing it on her apron and holding it up to the sky so that Benjamin could guess quite easily what it was. He moved back in case she would look up. She did not. He had imagined he would have felt differently about it. She disappeared into the kitchen and everything went on as before. He looked at the empty bird box and wondered without actually worrying about it, because he was still half thinking about the old lady, if in fact Mr Yates was all right.

It was a day peculiar with unhappened things. There was a feeling, because of the summery stillness and the cooking smells that were beginning to drift up from the lady's kitchen, that something would happen. In the same way with watching a pond: that sooner or later a minnow or a water boatman would ripple the surface.

It had been a peculiar day for the others.

Wilfred had brought home the pork meat from the Mayor's kitchen.

Paul had missed his tea.

Alice had seen him leaping across the brook.

The water from the boat had dripped on to Yanina's skirt.

Then in the late afternoon of this particular and most peculiar day, Benjamin found himself looking at Mr Yates!

It seemed as if he had been there a long time, but this could not have been so. Benjamin heard the old lady's back door closing. She always closed it at about this time.

Looking at Mr Yates, Benjamin felt as if the pigeon's eyes were going round and round. Songs of blackbirds and the sounds people make in the distances, all of it together, was going further and further away, as he looked at Mr Yates. Then the pigeon's grey skin lids closed. The spell was broken. Benjamin went to it and took the message from its foot.

He could take one thing. One thing only!

Well he would not take the marbles. He would leave them where they were, glinting on the window ledge. Remembering where they were he would be able to think of the beetly wood and the crickets and the old lady by her teapot, nodding off to sleep.

His father was delivering tables and the house was silent. Going downstairs, stopping sometimes so as to try to feel ordinary, he went to the hiding place. He was trembling in different parts, at the same time his thoughts were calm.

He put the bag of tools under his bed.

That is what he would take!

The message also said that he should have a good night's sleep.

This would be difficult.

Benjamin decided he would think of Mr Yates, imagining his eyes going round and round. That might do the trick!

6

Paul's Plan

LIKE A GULL CURLS ITS WINGS into the strong wind; past the sunny flints and turned earth: that was how Paul felt now!

He was standing on the town's river bridge, gripping the rail: eyes half closed. The bridge shook and quivered, as the vans and buses and people going home from work went over it. Perhaps he also felt as if he was on a ship shuddering down deep into a green wave hollow; crying "Steady as she goes!"

Paul was the leader, he told himself dreamily; a captain of children! Mr Yates had flown back to Benjamin, and there was Yanina! Paul had planned it carefully. Before sending the boat he had tested the course down the brook, putting a peeled twig in the water in Mabbs' field. He had run alongside it, waiting secretly at the end of Yanina's garden. The twig had finally arrived. There had been time for Paul to put his hand into the brook, feeling under the warm muddy roots at the side, for fish.

Now the last message to send was for Alice. He turned round to make sure no one was near him. The man who worked in the draper's shop where his father bought his silk waistcoats cycled by, wobbling as he smiled; raising his hat in greeting; nervous and anxious not to offend.

Then Paul practised an owl call. He was pleased with it. He felt hungry and light headed. The wind off the river ruffled and caressed him.

The river water was going by softly; swirling and spreading, almost stiffening here and there like a girl's head full of hair as she turns.

The town hall glistened in the late afternoon sun. Lines of

wires on poles stretched across in the distance and thousands of starlings circled; some of them starting to perch on the wires.

Paul hooted again.

There was only Alice! After that he must have a good night's sleep.

He was smiling; enjoying himself: staring into the distance. In the way that his mother would at times shut her eyes when talking to the Mayor, so Paul seemed to have eyes which could not be looked into. He hooted again, and looked at the town clock. He wondered what to do for the next hour until it was dark. Certainly he would have to wait because owls, generally speaking, did not hoot in the daylight.

7

Goose Fat, Silver Boots and Pig

WILFRED'S PRIMROSY WIFE had gone for ever when Alice was four. It was difficult for her to count back to it. If she struggled hard to do so her lips felt peculiar. In a peaceful lazy way she could go back to the number of times the apple tree had cropped: the one which overhung from the scrapyard.

She happened to remember it in this fashion because of a box of apples Wilfred had picked and the delicious smell from them. Alice was sitting on a rusty old cart in the scrapyard and had not been seen. The leather reins were green and rotted and fell apart as she thought of herself driving down the lanes and the wind whipping the clouds ahead of her. When she watched them finally leave, she had gone into the house and it was full of this apple smell.

Wilfred had been out all day cutting willow for his clothes pegs. Taking a little cheese with him wrapped in a red handkerchief; cooking it over a woodland fire. This was also to do with the apple time. It was cooler now in the late autumn days and Wilfred would have warmed his fingers by the flames.

Her mother came out with some old cases tied with string, then an armful of clothes. She was helped by a man who was a builder according to the name painted on the side of a van parked outside. He had a green hat. He threw the cases over the side of the van, on top of a wheelbarrow and some planks of wood. Before the van drove off, with the wheelbarrow bouncing up and down, Alice was close enough to notice what happened when her mother spoke. They were both laughing. Then as her mother spoke she could see the breath from her mouth as it became misty in the cool air. She had shivered as she watched. It was cool enough for the birds to have started to peck the apples which had not been gathered and rested red and yellow on the ground.

Afterwards Alice climbed up the stairs to their room at the top. A goose which had been cooked the day before had gone, although the jar full of goose fat had been left on the table. The tea pot was warm. When Wilfred returned, after thinking awhile, he made another pot of tea. Then he wrote a label for the jar. He stuck it on carefully. He did not seem too surprised at the thought of only the two of them being there.

Now Alice had this feeling of what it is like to be going. She was not going away for ever like her mother, or longer than even a day.

After seeing Paul leap the brook she sensed that the message would be sent soon now. She had found herself wondering what it had been like for her mother to be going, and indeed, whether she had made any more journeys away from other people, and whether she ever thought of the people in her life, who could not be touched any more.

The jar of goose fat was safely on the highest of three shelves. The label read 'Goose Fat' written in pen and ink with great care. It had never been touched, although several times Wilfred had mentioned that a little of it put on bread would have been very tasty.

Wilfred was dozing in the chair, his mouth flapping like the loose sails of a boat coming into the wind. Here and there, town lights, separated and spiky, shone in the evening mist. But in Mabbs' field and in the scrapyard it was all owly dark.

The downstairs back door opened on to a small back garden. Most of this was filled with pine trees planted to hide the old steam engines in the scrapyard. Their huge round bodies were green or rusty red colours and all of them were girdled with fine brass bands. There were old vans with solid rubber tyres; mangles for mangling clothes and old fashioned agricultural equipment like horse-drawn ploughs.

If Wilfred came-to suddenly from his sleep, because of living in the room at the top he would see none of this; only the pure skies and the stars or the oily clouds of winter and the rain lashing against the window panes. This, more than anything else made him think of the places where he had been, often making him sleep again.

Alice was able to walk under the trees except where the dead lower branches had laced together. Most of the time it was dry under the pine trees, even when it was raining hard with no birds singing. It always smelled of resin.

The special place where the message would be put was on a nail driven into one of the pine trees. Some resin had formed where the nail had entered the tree. It was clear and valuable looking, like an amber bead.

She had been coming out of the butcher's with bones for soup. "You're the pegmaker's girl."

Alice turned. It was more of an accusation: not a question.

"Yes, I am," she said, her shoulders hardening with anger. "Who are you?"

She had looked into the stony ground of Paul's eyes without wavering.

"Benjamin, the tablemaker's son, said you would like to come with us."

Alice shrugged.

"If you do," said Paul, "you must do something brave as well."

"Then tell me," said Alice.

"The owls come to the pine trees in your patch don't they?"

"It's a garden," said Alice.

"Well all right," Paul said, "I will deliver the message one night soon. I will hoot like an owl."

"That's not very frightening," Alice said.

"Where can I put the message?"

"There's a nail in a tree," Alice replied. "I will tie a rag to it."

"It may be a real owl or just me. You won't know. And each night you must take your guinea pig with you."

"How do you know I've got a guinea pig?"

"I do know. That's what matters. So you will have to protect your pig. Is that frightening enough for you?" Paul smiled. But his eyes did not light up.

She said "It will be. A little."

For several nights she had gone to the pines as agreed. Sometimes they creaked and groaned, the branches tugging at each other. Or they were very still and black against the sky.

Although the nights were warm and summery and the crickets chirped Alice often started to shiver. She never took her eyes off her pig. Sometimes it would whistle with alarm. She kept it in a box.

They were all real owls and at the end of each vigil there had been no message on the nail.

On this particular and special night: its particularity made more so because of the flapping of Wilfred's mouth as his wild dreaming took him on kettle-looking walks: this night Alice decided about the guinea pig. She would let it out to move a little at her feet, on the dry bed of pine needles.

From some cardboard she cut out the shape of a large Arabian or Indian looking knife. Her fingers burned where the scissors had dug in. Then she went to the cupboard where Wilfred kept his boots, his brushes, and the pot of silver paint. She painted the knife until it gleamed. Then she wiped the brush dry on Wilfred's boots. The knife was then glued to the end of a pole and tied with string.

Alice stood in the clearing by the pine trees. She trembled in the warm, cricket-chirruping night. There was no moon, but enough light from the stars to make the knife glint; and in it so doing, she felt brave in spite of her trembling. The guinea pig did not move far from her feet. The pine needles were of no interest to it, but it was whistling softly. On the end of the pole she had tied an old dressing-gown tassle of Wilfred's. Alice would not be afraid!

She looked up to where one of the new airliners droned across the sky. Its lights shone for a long time, furrowing the sky like old farming tackle did: brushing and cutting the earth. She looked into the dark sky and imagined, far away, the fierce winds on the edge of the world.

Once a real owl hooted; full of broken mice. This owl would be wise, she said to herself, and leave the pig alone! She gripped the handle of the pole tightly, ready to use it. Her nostrils were hard and the shaking had stopped.

The pig started to whistle and to scramble about in the pine

needles. Then there were three owl noises, long and drawn
out: wavering on the dying notes: sounding worse than any
real owl she had ever heard.

"You dare!" she shouted. "You dare!" The knife gleamed
dully, Wilfred's tassle quivering as she stood her ground. She
stood as the guards of Rome must have done or the Arabian
princes, by their tents in the dark desert.

The end of her nose was cold. There was a cracking of dry
twigs. She counted up to twenty and then went to the tree
with the nail in it.

Wilfred had gone to sleep in his chair as he sometimes did,
although he had a bed. When he was remembering about
being on the road it suited him to be in the chair; falling
asleep, waking up suddenly, startled. Often there had been a
policeman waking him up on a bench, saying "Come along
there! Move along!" Waking up startled with dreams, he
would know little by little that he was in his own chair; that he
could stay there until the dawn and no policeman however
large could ask him to move from it. Knowing this gave him
such a feeling of satisfaction that he would often not use his
bed.

Alice looked at him, then gently put a blanket over his
shoulders. She put the pig in his hut by the cupboard. She lay
down by the empty fireplace, on a horsehair mattress. She got
up once to make sure there was enough bread in the bin for
Wilfred for the next day.

She knew she was a half gypsy. Sometimes it made her
secretly proud. She thought it was a gypsy trick she had that
she could go to sleep quickly by getting the feeling of walking
ahead on paths where no one had ever been before.

Some of the message ordered her to have a good night's
sleep.

She knew straight away what the 'one thing only' would be.
She would take her guinea pig!

The room still smelled of the silver paint. The smell would
be gone, she told herself, by the morning.

8

Gathering in a Secret Place

THEY WENT IN THE EARLY MORNING; first gathering in a secret place in Mabbs' yard, in an old chicken hut.

Yanina came to it by walking along the brook, past Mr Carey's strawberries and the alert beetles in the grasses.

Benjamin took a pathway that led him to the field, past Mr Mabbs' horse, white and friendly, whinnying softly in the early morning light with no flies to torment it.

Alice came to the place the special way, carrying her pig in one arm and a bottle of water. She trod with care over boxes of empty medicine bottles. The wooden cases were green and slippery; then she went under the archways of ivy that had grown over the unwanted scrap iron. Elder bushes were growing everywhere. Huge flies stayed in the light streams that shone through the trees; their green and blue wings winking for a moment, then gone.

Now in front of her was the chicken hut.

After all the waiting, after standing under the pines, she was at last going to the most important meeting yet.

Paul was coming to it by the road, as Benjamin and Yanina had done after they had crossed Mabbs' field.

Benjamin had opened his tool bag and the tools were spread out on the floor.

Paul said to Alice: "You're late." Then, "Does anyone want any cocoa before we go?"

"If we light a fire here we will be seen," said Yanina.

"I've thought of that," Paul replied. "It would take ages for anyone to reach us the way Alice came and no one knows of the way through the fence."

"Well I don't want any," said Benjamin.

"Alice?"

Then Alice's pig whistled.

Paul looked at the box, shaking his head. "Oh well, we can all see what Alice chose to bring with her! Yanina, you can carry the water. All of you come on. It's time to go." He stood by the fence, moving the loose board so that he could look out. "You know what to do. Just walk slowly and we'll join up at the end of the street." He signalled Benjamin and tapped him on the back. Then he did the same to Yanina.

Waiting by them, wishing she had drunk some cocoa because of the early morning cold, Alice asked Paul, "How long will the journey be?"

He did not answer. It was all happening so fast: as if nothing could be stopped.

"How long do you think?" Alice repeated.

Paul tapped her on the shoulder.

It was like leaving a shore; with Paul being the sailor man at the helm in his blue jersey and cap who talks to no one.

Alice first noticed the peculiar feeling as she walked by the doors of the roadside cottages. Some of them had small gardens, but most of the doors opened on to the road. It was too early for many people to be about. An old man in a cloth cap stood by his garden gate, his back turned, pruning roses.

The door of a bakery opened and along the pavement they walked through the smell of bread. Alice could see the back of a man as he worked at a table, shaping the dough.

Past the doors of these people she felt the presence of the homes and small shops like a spirit troubling her. Many of the doors were opened. Some only enough for a hand to reach in; just enough to see the colours of brass and copper and green tablecloths, black grates; to smell the gentle smell off the surface of nuts in bowls and the strong geranium smell and the clothes of the people.

But there was not one turned face!

Dragging behind Paul and Yanina and leaving Benjamin ahead of her with his bag of tools, she stopped at one wide open door. A lady was standing over her stove. Alice stood on the steps feeling light in the head. The lady was making a suet pudding. The side of her face and neck was red and steamy as well; the bag of suet bumping up and down in the pot of boiling water.

No one had looked at them!

"Come on!" It was Paul. He was pulling at her arm.

They were going into the New World, she told herself, leaving the pavements and funny houses. They were going to the woods where the green back of the grasshopper would rest in the sun, his hopping legs still, and the rabbit would think of the clump of bracken in front of it.

"Alice! Alice!"

Paul took her down, leading her to the pavement, past all the cottages and old shops with drawers of whatever they were selling and tills which would later sound like the ringing of ships bells; past the cottagers' hissing kettles.

Once Alice thought she saw the motherly face of a lady turning to her in the shadows of her kitchen; her face alight with smiles and just as suddenly, then, the vision of it had plunged into darkness like the wings of coloured flies had ebbed to nothing so quickly in the sunlight in Mabbs' yard.

The gaps between the cottages grew. They passed a field of weeds, waist high with yellow flowers. In the distance, above the morning mist, were the hills and the woods. The sun was in their noses now. They walked away from the houses by the small hedged fields, choked with the blossom of buttercup and clover. Benjamin had dropped behind Paul and Yanina. He shifted the tool bag from one hand to the other.

From behind him Alice called, "I will help you." She had been sent to the back by Paul, out of their hearing.

Benjamin said in a voice soft with shame: "I can't understand him minding the whistling. I think you are very lucky to have — a pig."

As Alice took the other handle of the tool bag so that it swung between them, she asked Benjamin, thinking that perhaps he had an answer, "How long do you think it will be?"

"You see," she added, "I put on a bit of paper 'back soon'."

It was on the table, in their room.

"Then that will be all right. I suppose it will," said Benjamin.

As the lane wound into the hillside its banks deepened. Camomile and grass grew in the road centre because it was so little used. Paul said: "There are not many people here. A farmcart comes along maybe. But one of the ideas is that we should not be seen. So we must leave the road."

"Where does it go?" asked Benjamin.

"It stops short of the woods. But we go to them another way."

They climbed the bank. In the distance the trees glistened in the morning sun. Yanina thought 'I wish I had brought the telescope'.

Black crows looked still in the sky because of their great distance. She thought of the sea birds Uncle Stephen would have seen with it and the decks of junks in the lazy China Sea, all shining with light: trying to see the look on the faces of the people.

"Come on!" said Paul nudging her. "This is the way."

Once they followed a footpath through the ripening corn. It was just higher than Paul's head. But Alice, who was the shortest, walking behind the rest, was deep down in the swaying green and gold of the field. They went along by hedges of different colours, through poppy fields, often startling larks into the sky, where they sang.

"Pig," said Alice, "I will tie your box over my back."

Benjamin made holes in the side of the box with a gimlet for the string. The pig's box was pressed close to Alice's back. Now, the white and black flintstones on the field edges and the flocks of untroubled peewits bounced up and down for the surprised pig, as Alice walked; and the pig was quiet at last.

"There is one more resting place after this," said Paul as they gathered round an old hedgerow tree. From a hole in its rotten stump he took a tin of cocoa and an iron pot.

Alice searched for kindling and then watched Yanina try to light the fire.

"Let Alice do it," said Benjamin. "I've seen her: she can do it."

Paul smiled. "I expect it comes naturally."

"It's easy enough," said Alice quickly, her fingers hurting with the sticks which she broke again and again.

Yanina made the cocoa. Some of the milk had spilled in Paul's bag and it was spread out in the sun to dry. She smiled at Alice saying "Do you take sugar?"

Just like a lady being kind, like the preacher's wife, thought Alice.

"'Course I do," said Alice. Then she went on: "Yes I know about looking for wood and things like that you don't know."

Yanina was stirring her cup, looking into it. Paul was slumped back against the tree and Benjamin was nearly asleep. Paul prodded Benjamin, "Didn't I say get a good night's sleep?"

"I did," he mumbled.

"Well come on then."

Alice walked with Benjamin, helping him again with the bag of tools. They came near to the last resting place before the woods. She could smell the lavender scent. "Why did you bring it?" she asked.

"I can think of things."

"What sort?"

"Well Mr Carey for instance bending down for water in the brook to put on the strawberries."

In front of them they all looked for an instant into the eyes of a stoat jewelled with knowing of the rabbit ahead of it.

Paul turned on Alice.

"All right then. Why on earth did you bring a pig?"

"You said anything." Alice replied.

"And it's no trouble," Benjamin said.

"I'll tell you a thing," said Alice, "about Pig. He'll be at home tonight. Not in a dark smelly old wood."

"That's what I mean," said Paul. "It's making up your mind for you."

"I know," said Alice, the colour patches showing on her cheeks, "where I'm going to be as well, even if there wasn't Pig."

"And you," taunted Paul, "you Benjamin! What do you miss? It's not the end of the morning yet. Come on, what do you miss already?"

"Nothing really," said Benjamin.

"Foxes cough in the dark in the woods and the grounds gets smelly," murmured Alice.

"I wish I'd brought the marbles and not the tool bag. And I've thought of the old lady below and the bacon she cooks but that's all. I haven't missed anything. I'm glad I'm here."

"We must go to the end of the woods," Paul said.

Two fields away the treetops glistened, darkening again for a moment as clouds covered the sun.

"We planned it for ages," said Yanina, "polishing the stair rail, listening to my aunt, you've no idea!"

"Oh yes we have," said Paul. "What about my father? Anybody want my father?"

"No thanks," said Benjamin.

Yanina said, looking into the hedge, "This is the last resting place, isn't it?" Although she had walked some of the way with Paul a few days before, hiding the supplies in old tree stumps or rabbit holes, she did not want to make him feel any less of a leader. So she asked, knowing it was.

"But it's gone," she said. "Paul, there's no cocoa here. There's nothing. I know this was the place."

"I'm thirsty," said Benjamin.

"There's a stream in the wood," said Paul grimly. "I wonder who . . . ?"

Yanina turned and saw the man in the hazel trees, standing on the wild garlic, crushed with his boots, and the garlic smelling. He just looked at them, with a soft smile on his face as if he had been waiting for them for days. Like the sort of look on a keeper's face as he bent down to a rabbit.

Paul grunted because of the speed at which he started to run. Yanina raced like a deer. Benjamin was in front of Alice, his arms raised curiously high with the burst of running, as if he was pushing the air in front of him as he struggled to get away.

His hands, thought Alice and stopped. Oh Benjamin! Benjamin!

She turned and walked. There was no sound of running feet behind her. So they must have stopped; watching.

The man stayed where he was. He looked surprised. He

tried to hide this by fumbling with his hand over his mouth. He made no move.

She stopped by Benjamin's bag, still looking into the man's blackberry-coloured eyes. Then she stooped, grasped the bag and ran as she had never run before.

A cloud cleared from the sun and its shadows sped across the woodland slopes.

"Here we are! This way Alice!"

"Well," said Paul, when they were all safely in the woods, "that was pretty brave."

"Is your pig all right?" asked Yanina.

"Yes I think so. Now," she said. Turning to Paul, "I know we'll be here a little while. Then I will leave for to get back in time for tea."

"I'm the leader," said Paul.

"I'm Alice," said Alice, "and I'm not being awkward. But it's then for certain and not later."

"Oh all right. Very well. In that case we must all look for the path."

9

As a Girl with No Shame would Feel

"WHAT IS IT LIKE?" asked Benjamin.

"It's an ordinary path . . . yet!" Paul said. "The thing about it is that you forget things."

"Don't be silly," said Yanina.

"Wait and see. You haven't been this far. For instance Ben you'll feel as if your parents never existed. At any rate that's how I feel. I couldn't remember my father being angry."

Yanina had broken a toadstool. "That's the colour of him when he's like that," said Paul.

"It's poisonous," said Yanina, and crushed it into the leaves.

"D'you know I think none of you likes your parents," said Alice.

"She is my aunt," said Yanina.

"All right, your aunt."

"And you will forget all about Wilfred," said Paul.

"What is wrong with my father?" asked Alice. She turned facing them, looking into their faces and said quietly: "There's nothing wrong with my father."

They stopped. The woods seemed to grow dark. The wind fled through the high branches. In a clearing a rabbit, alert with fear, stopped brushing its face with a paw and looked towards them.

"That's what we all have in common, about our parents. It's why we're here," Paul muttered.

His voice seemed to come from a long distance. They went on talking about him. Paul was saying: "And your father has taken food from my kitchen."

"Given it!" said Alice feeling light-headed.

Yanina joined in. "He plays a flute and hangs about outside shops and almost begs, doesn't he?"

Benjamin looked at Alice: "Well I have never seen it."

"Not that you would," Paul replied, "with your Mr Yates: waiting and waiting."

Alice looked into Paul's eyes, which she did sometimes to find out if she would again get this curious feeling. This time it was like the sea on an empty sort of day, pulling over the rocks.

"My father tells people," went on Paul, "that people like Wilfred are a threat to ordinary people."

"Why?" asked Alice.

"Because he paints his boots silver for example," said Yanina.

Shame rolled upon Alice, and she could not stop it. Benjamin had said gently to her, "We had best get on I think." But she stood there.

She saw a beady-eyed raven sitting on a tree stump close to them. Wilfred had noticed things like that, on walks, and the way the breeze ruffled the back feathers. By the stump was the overgrown entrance to a path. There was light about it: a mistiness, where the circles and coins of light scattered down from the swaying tree-tops. Still the feeling of shame about the boots! Remembering how she had been looking at the cat in the window as her father had cut the hedges. No, she had cried, he is not my father.

As she looked into the eye of the raven she felt as if she was about to enter a garden. As a girl with no shame would feel, entering a garden of many flowers, dressed in a fine dress, with gravel paths and cut grass lawns and unwanted jellies left on the table from tea.

Paul said softly: "Be quiet both of you. She has seen that path. This time I did not see it."

"How do you know?" Benjamin whispered.

"Be quiet and follow her."

The dewey-eyed raven flew into the green heights, by the lumbering branches where no people had ever been; and higher still where the sunlight bristled on the hills. Light streamed in where an old tree had groaned and crashed to the ground.

Then as the sky clouded over they could see more into the shadows. The calls of birds, restive before rain, filled the woodland air. Paul's step had become uncertain. The pig was whistling, as if he too understood that there was to be a storm. Now and then large drops of rain splashed down.

Paul said: "I haven't been this far before."

But Alice walked on.

"If you are thinking about tea?" said Paul.

Benjamin, carrying the bag alone because of the narrow path, slid past Paul and Yanina, to be behind Alice.

The wind which had now gathered ahead of the rain storm made a sound in the trees, which made him shiver. It was like the sea and the sound of many horsemen galloping over fields which were far away.

Almost as a red-eyed jungle animal might go plunging through the vines and orchids: so Alice led them!

They had all stopped breathless. Alice was gulping lightly, her nostrils dilated. "There is a little further to go. We are near the end."

Paul muttered. "I say we go back now. I am the leader."

"We know that," said Yanina, adding "You are not afraid are you?"

"I am not!" said Paul. "The path has ended and I must think of other people's safety!"

Benjamin was looking at Yanina. Their eyes met. He gave her a long wink. Then he blushed deeply.

Alice said in a voice thick with excitement, "But look, I was right! There!"

Stumbling, they ran towards the building. Benjamin held back for an instant calling out "Wait, let's think."

The light started to fail as the last storm clouds knitted together. The rain fell steadily through the leaves; running in rivulets down the boles of trees.

They stopped short of it.

"Look, there are sacks in the windows," Yanina whispered.

"It's very old-looking," Benjamin said.

Paul said "I've no doubt it was once a woodman's cottage."

"I never heard of a woodman in a wood like this," replied Benjamin.

"Well you don't know everything. So now we can go back."

But Alice ran across the clearing. Then Yanina joined her, followed by Benjamin. They stood in the crumbling old porch.

"It hasn't got a door," Benjamin said.

Now it rained in earnest. Paul's face almost disappeared.

"Come on, run!"

"Here," said Yanina as he joined them, his teeth chattering. He was clasping his hands, and he was bent down stiffly with the sudden drenching; not able to speak.

Yanina pulled one of the sacks from the window frame and rubbed him down with it. "There," she said, "is that better?"

"I'm all right," said Paul.

"Where are we?" asked Benjamin.

"I don't know," said Alice in a normal-sounding, worried, thin sort of voice, adding "I must be back in time for tea."

A weak-looking elder bush grew in the middle of the kitchen floor, struggling towards a gaping hole in the roof. Far above them green leaves twisted and shuddered, glowing and shifting in the gloom. Alice's cheeks looked pinched as she worried about tea.

Benjamin picked up an iron mug covered in green moss. "Well at least people have been here."

Paul, who had been moving cautiously about, trying cupboard doors, looking into dark gaps, suddenly picked up an iron rod. He raised it above his head, swinging it round and round. "There's no one here now!"

The rain was falling steadily. "So why are you afraid?" he shouted. He hit the elder bush. "No one, no one, no one here!" By now the branches were struck down at his feet.

Yanina said "I have found something. Look."

At first they did not hear her.

"Paul," Yanina called, "how many candles have you?"

"Three," he answered.

"Well if one of us walks in the dark behind the rest it will be all right."

"What do you mean?" asked Benjamin.

"It isn't a cupboard door at all. It leads somewhere."

"Wait," Paul said, "can anybody hear anything?"

They were standing in a passageway.

"No I can't," said Alice, "but there's a feeling. I think it's only because I'm tired. I feel shivery because of it."

She was tired like the preacher after a sermon, or like Wilfred after cutting pegwood with an aching back and a trickle of sweat going into his eye. After leading them through the woods, there seemed nothing left, only tiredness and a feeling of something over and done with forever. She was glad to be at the back; the one without a candle so that she could be alone. She carried Benjamin's tool bag. The distance between Alice and the others lengthened and she felt drowsy, brought to her senses for a moment by the sudden squeaking of her pig.

Benjamin was calling back. "Alice. Are you all right?"

She could hear the high-pitched squeak of bats, but she was not afraid. It was as if she was resting safely on a ledge, unmindful of the eagles that moved slowly beneath her. The glow of candle light moved fitfully. The passage walls had vanished.

"Where's Alice?" Paul asked.

"Here I am."

"We're standing in a large room," said Yanina. Then there were more corridors. They went seeking down them like bees trembling on blossoms of light, casting yellow haloes with their candles. Sometimes they would stand back in wonder at the sight of a high broken roof where the woodland light streamed in.

Benjamin's eyes were bright with excitement. "Are you all right now?" he asked Alice.

The rain had stopped. In the next room the whole roof had fallen in. The rain was steaming off the mass of broken tiles and rotten timber. Birds sang with that strange passion they seem to feel after a storm. Glassy-looking forms sprouted from the walls. There were mosses of tranquil greens.

"It's more like an old mansion," said Paul.

"Shall we go on?" asked Yanina pointing to another passageway.

Alice turned to look back. On the corner of the wall was the remains of a stone gargoyle. There was moss on one side of his face.

Further on there were some stone steps.

Paul had started to unpack food.

Yanina and Alice climbed them.

"It's slippery, watch out!" warned Alice.

Then they came to the edge, gasping with surprise.

The roof above them was without tiles.

"Come on," called Paul, "food's ready." Then, "Where are you?"

"We must be very careful going down," whispered Yanina.

"Someone lives here," was all Alice could say.

Sunlight was filtering into the wood. The clearing beneath the window was bright and tinkling with draining storm water. Marrows were there with gold and green streaks and there were lines of gooseberry bushes. Clinging to the wall, coming up to the window, was a rose of deep red, of a beauty Alice had never known before.

"It's all so strange. Be very careful coming down," said Yanina.

10

Lord Augustus

"I WAS HUNGRY." Benjamin looked at the bread and jam sandwiches with distaste.

Alice said: "There's someone living here. We saw it up there."

"Do you want any sandwiches or don't you?" Paul asked impatiently.

"Not really." Benjamin turned to Alice. "I don't think anyone would live here."

"Well you didn't see the rows of gooseberry bushes. Or the marrows," said Alice.

"There is a most peculiar smell," Yanina interrupted, as she was about to eat her sandwiches. "I don't think it's in the sandwich. It's everywhere isn't it? Can you smell it?"

Benjamin took a sandwich. "It's not more in the sandwich than it is anywhere else."

"It's a dog smell," said Alice, "and look."

It came out of the shadows in a series of runs. It would stop and look at them and then sidle up closer to them. It was an ugly dog with very little hair and crooked legs. Its nose was flat. A fresh looking pink tongue poked out from the centre of its mouth. It came close to Benjamin who said "Oh my goodness!" and gave the dog his sandwich, moving away as he did so.

"It is probably quite friendly," said Alice, as she threw her sandwich on the ground.

Paul finished his defiantly. "Next time someone else can make them."

"There's some paper twisted around his collar," Benjamin said.

Alice bent down. The dog looked at her with his coal black eyes. The tongue moved quickly in and out. Yanina started laughing.

"All it says is 'Follow'. Just that!"

"Why not then?" said Yanina.

The dog moved towards the entrance to the last unexplored room and they followed it.

Alice and Yanina screamed almost at the same time. Benjamin made no sound. But his candle was shaking so much it looked as if his face was moving with the constant shifting of light and shadow. Then Paul too saw the face.

The most remarkable thing about it was the nose. It stood out in the candle glow.

A voice spoke.

"I did not mean to frighten you." A hand faltered over his face like a black spider. "My trouble is I have a fatty nose. I have always had a fatty nose."

Although there was a hard edge to it, Yanina laughed again as if she was not able to stop it.

As the man lit a lamp, his features suddenly came into relief. The nose was remarkable and not just because of its length or its fattiness which made it gleam like a reflected moon in a night-time pond. It was because his eyes were so obscured with bushy eyebrows and his face and head so covered with hair that his nose became the centre of attention.

In fact it seemed the only clear part of him left.

"There," he said as he adjusted the wick. "I saw you coming. I have prepared one or two things as you will notice."

At first Alice could not quite see what was there.

A pot of cold potatoes, which did not look appetising at all, and, most decidedly, a half-eaten gooseberry pie. Although she liked gooseberries, her stomach was feeling tight and she could not bear the thought of food just yet. Besides, the dog was sitting by her stool with its very strong dog smell.

"The lamp smokes a bit," the man said.

Alice hoped it would go on smoking as it was gradually masking the smell of dog. The dog would not take his eyes off her. No one was saying anything yet. She knew Paul was struggling to say something suitable because of being the leader. The dog's eyes were glinting like stone: like sharply polished flints.

The man was pouring tea into some old tin mugs. He tapped Alice's mug, then in front of her unbelieving eyes he picked off a stubborn piece of moss.

Yanina's mug leaked. A jet of tea poured on to the floor.

"Share with the boy," he said, pointing to Paul.

At last Paul spoke. "You are very kind, Sir."

Then the others talked. Alice had the persistent and peculiar feeling of watching them talk, without it seeming to make anything more real. She knew Paul had mentioned about being kind.

The man was talking to her. They were all looking at her now. She felt the hot tin mug against her mouth.

"What is *your* name?"

She felt he must have asked for it before. With great effort she said "Alice."

Then Benjamin said to the man, "What is *your* name?"

Yanina smiled nervously. She said quietly in a voice that clearly showed he should not have asked it, "Benjamin!"

The pause was long and uncomfortable.

"What do you call your guinea pig?"

"She just calls it Pig," said Yanina.

"That's not very good," he said.

"He seems to answer to it," she replied.

"Have you a pet?" he asked Benjamin.

"Yes I have, Sir."

"And what do you call him?"

"Mr Yates. He's a pigeon."

"Now that is good!"

He had pushed the lamp further away because of the smelly wick.

"What would you call me," he went on, "if I had no name?"

"No name!" he said again his voice echoing in the hollow roof.

Alice heard a commotion coming from the dark. It was a sound she had heard before in some of the places and old buildings she had been to with Wilfred on peg-cutting journeys. It did not worry her. The others did not even hear it.

It was coming from the bats, dislodged, quivering, aghast at the patch of lamplight beneath them.

Benjamin answered him.

As he did so, he felt as he had done in the cellar of his home with the afternoon light streaming onto his table. It was as if he had entered again into some strange vale of knowledge for an instant.

He spoke without thinking; with certainty: afterwards puzzled and surprised at himself.

"Lord Augustus!"

"You're absolutely right!" he said straight away, "absolutely right!"

He stroked his nose.

"I am — " he paused, "Lord Augustus."

*   *   *

Then the food was passed round. Paul helped himself, seemingly unaware of the reek of cold potato. Alice quickly gave hers to the dog, hoping that it would go. It just gulped and looked at her steadily again, with the sort of stare a person might use who had been given the wrong change.

Lord Augustus reached over with the teapot. She had never seen such a hairy man. But he seemed very kind.

"There," he said, "it will do you good. Would you like a little gooseberry pie?"

The tea had eased the gripping feeling in Alice's stomach. But the voices still seemed far away. "Just a little," said Alice faintly. Thinking perhaps she had not been heard, she cleared her throat and looking into his half-hidden eyes said again, most distinctly, "A little please."

Lord Augustus ran his thumb down his nose.

"The dog is not troubling you?"

"No, Sir."

Turning to Benjamin he went on. "So you spend your time in the pigeon loft?"

"I do. Yes."

"And now," said Lord Augustus quietly having listened to Benjamin, "I will tell you about yourself and this Mr Yates. Think of him with his breast feathers pressed flat as he hurtles over the cottages and fields; tumbling over the cold churches and the mice nosing at cheese; over the fish in the shady river water! You can't do that! Mr Yates must feel sorry for you! Waiting and waiting, all alone, away from your kind. Be less with your Mr Yates. He needs you less than you think. In fact maybe I think it is not at all. I think maybe he doesn't need you at all except for the provision of corn."

"That's not true," whispered Benjamin. "I give him food!"

But Lord Augustus went on. "So he needs you for the food and the box to sleep in. You should see less of him that is all." Then he changed the subject abruptly. "I'll tell you what. You have run away for the day haven't you?" Lord Augustus looked around the table. Seeing Yanina's tin mug was empty he lifted the teapot but she quickly put her hand over her mug shaking her head.

"You have, all of you for that matter from what I have heard, run away for the day?"

The smell of the lamp was making Alice sleepy.

"Otherwise you would not be here," he went on quietly, "and I wouldn't be talking to you, would I?"

"No you wouldn't," Alice agreed since he was looking at her. She drank some of the fresh tea, but the inside of the mug still smelled like a shed that had been closed for the winter.

"My boy," said Lord Augustus, "clean the van. Without being told. Don't expect results too soon, but all the same clean the van."

"The inside or the outside?" asked Benjamin, more to humour him.

"Start with the outside. Do it until you can see your face in it."

Then he heard about Yanina and her aunt and Mr Carey wearing his broken straw hat and coarse gardening trousers bending down in his vegetable garden and about his fingers getting stained dull red with strawberries. Yanina told him of the brook at the bottom of the garden and the boat with the message in it from Paul and about the shallow brook water sliding over the stones the colour of woodlice.

"What did you bring?" Lord Augustus asked.

"The lavender scent Mr Carey gave me."

"And he will be anxious for you, like a bird for bread."

"I don't think my aunt . . ." Yanina began.

"What don't you think? I ask you! Of course she will be anxious. Don't you think Uncle Stephen and the way he died, with his head full of what to eat for the day, had something to do with her being bitter like a crab apple I don't doubt."

"She is *rather*," Yanina agreed.

"He is thinking only about food. Then the seas alter and the storm drowns him. Pfhut!"

"What do you mean?"

"By Pfhut? All gone! No more holidays on shore and pots of tea; listening to him. And the fruit of all this feeling, wrenching out, are the crab apples."

"It was only for the day anyway," said Yanina. "We were only running away for today."

"Alice has got to be back for tea," said Benjamin.

"Polish Uncle Stephen's telescope," said Lord Augustus.

"It seems to me," said Paul, who had lost all nervousness, "that your answer to everything is polishing."

Lord Augustus looked at him steadily for a moment. Then he spoke to Yanina. "Take her a cup of tea in bed. See what happens."

"I am not very hopeful," she said quietly.

Paul interrupted. "I don't think your name is Lord Augustus at all."

"Don't you? It is not necessary for you to believe this. For I have nothing to say to you. I am standing at the shore line when I look at you. The tide has sucked away all the pink shells. I see nothing."

Alice knew what he meant! Because so often she had the same feelings.

"Except that one day you will have as much if not more than your father."

The strength of a lion! Leaping over the brook! Mabbs' old horse looking, shaking its head, then bending down again.

You are nothing but an old tramp, Paul thought. You are not Lord Augustus. Just as Mr Yates is not really Mr Yates, but only a silly old bird.

More gooseberry pie was passed round.

Lord Augustus said "Empty your mugs," tipping his own

on the floor, then knocking the mug on the side of the table to get rid of the tea leaves. He poured a little wine in each. Benjamin gave Yanina his mug.

"There, a spoonful each. It will do no harm. And you can drink it in thankfulness."

Paul asked "What for?"

Yanina looked crossly at Paul and taking her mug, drank from it and said "Thank you Lord Augustus."

"And *you* my dear," he nodded and turned to Alice. "There's only you left to talk about."

"Thank you very much," she said, "but I left a note saying I would be back for tea, and I don't think . . ."

"She does not think there is time," said Benjamin.

"Oh there is time. Oh yes," Lord Augustus fingered his nose, "and you will be back in time for tea."

"We are not sure of the way back," said Yanina.

"You see, you don't go back that way. We are near the edge of the wood. All you do is go through the door over there. That leads you into the garden."

"We've been walking through the woods for at least an hour," Paul said.

"Ah, so you have," Lord Augustus replied. "Now you go just past the gooseberries into the woods for a minute: past a hollow oak tree; then — pfhut!"

Alice thought dreamily to herself. Why don't we sit where the bushes are and the stripey marrows and the greenfinches and the other birds clasping the damp boughs. Lord Augustus was saying: "Benjamin, as you go by the hollow tree, put your tools in it. They will keep dry. You can come back to it and build a hut of hazel and gathered branches. You can build a fine hut in the summer now, from the sappy wood and the sap will run down your wrist."

"But can we come here again?" asked Yanina.

"It will be difficult to find except by the way you got here."

"Then I will build a hazel hut," said Benjamin.

In between listening to them, Alice thought of the roses outside the window and the silvery green gooseberries. She said "Why can't we go out into the sun?"

But Lord Augustus said only to her, "You did not want to

run away for the day?"

"No I did not. But if I am back . . ."

"Your father is a fine man from accounts."

"People know him in the town and in places about," said Alice.

"He scavenges," said Paul, "and gets meat from my father's kitchen."

Alice stood up, her head light with anger.

The dog's tongue was popping in and out, and from where she was standing now she could get a terrible dog smell of ragged collars and ears and old fur. Lord Augustus was smiling gently. The dog was now going round and round in circles, chasing its tail. Paul was talking.

But for Alice, all sound seemed to have gone, Lord Augustus clapped his hands; and long afterwards Alice remembered that she did not even hear that.

*   *   *

Lord Augustus was breathing in deeply; like a frog in the marshes, ready to croak. A fear came upon Alice. The others did not seem to be moving: their faces fixed in different ways. Oh how she wanted to be in the safety of the corn field again, with the corn higher than her head and the blazing red poppies and the hard rutty ground!

Then Lord Augustus clapped his hands again and it seemed to Alice that his hands came together very slowly and when they met there was enough time to think about how it had been the last time she and Wilfred were out gathering peg wood. Then the sound came to her.

Then quickening, spinning round in the well-like silence, she heard another noise. The dog was sucking his tongue in and out. Lord Augustus was smiling and nodding at Alice. She heard a flute playing. Her pig spun around in its box squeaking. Then the noise of the flute she knew so well filled Alice's head, drowning the pig's noise; although its pink lips were rounded with the might of the sound it was making, like a lady opera singer.

Lord Augustus had moved away from the lamplight. Then, because of the shadows he would sometimes appear to vanish altogether. In this strange darkness, like an ocean deep, she was certain she once saw Wilfred's face. The flute playing became wilder and then without thinking about whether it was a sensible thing to do or not, Alice climbed on to the table and danced.

She remembered the lamp swaying and Yanina holding it so that it would not fall down. Benjamin was laughing. In her thoughts about it: remembering it often as she grew older, Alice would also recall the bats. In spite of the pig whistling away and the wild sound of Wilfred's flute, she heard also, thinking about it for an instant only, the squeaking of the bats.

Straight away a coldness went into her and she stood still. She could no longer see Lord Augustus. Benjamin and Paul and Yanina were sitting at the table their faces marbled in silence. Even the dog seemed to have gone, although there was still a strong smell of it. Alice climbed down awkwardly.

Even Pig has gone quiet, she thought, and turned the box around and looked into it and saw Pig huddled deep in the straw. Alice put a fist to her eye to grub out the beginning of a tear.

Yanina was the first to move. The lamp was nearly out and smoking badly, so she took a candle with her to the door.

"Help me," she called to Benjamin as she struggled to open it. Then it gave way and her hair and skin was alive with sunlight.

Alice rushed out past her. "Oh look!" she called to Yanina. "It's all as we saw it."

Benjamin was bending down by the gooseberry bushes feeling the warm hairy clusters of fruit. Yanina had gone back to the door. "Where are you?" she called. Then thinking perhaps he had followed behind them, although it seemed most unlikely, she returned outside to the clearing and called again.

"Lord Augustus!"

All about them the trees tumbled into the sky. At the sound of her voice a bird fled from its perch on a beech bough. Yanina walked on the soft grass beyond the marrows and the gooseberries, where it became wild again. There were rabbit droppings everywhere.

"The animals have left the marrows alone," she said.

"I'm warm," said Benjamin.

Now Paul called, clearing his throat two or three times: "Lord Augustus!"

"Oh well," he said, his voice sounding higher than usual, "I suppose we'd better find the path."

"Just do what he said," Yanina spoke, leading them past the gooseberries.

"They are very ripe and nice," said Benjamin.

Taking his hand for a moment, Yanina said "Benjamin come along. We must all go back now. We must keep the bushes on our right."

Again Paul called out: "Lord Augustus!"

Yanina looked at him steadily. "He has gone. He was just an old tramp as you said, I expect."

"I think he has gone," said Alice, "and everything else has stopped." She was going to discuss what she meant, but did not, needing more time to think about it. Somehow, she promised herself, she would have to find out if the others had heard and seen as she had done.

PART TWO

11

The Back Door

BENJAMIN SHOUTED "Here it is!" He climbed into the tree and sat on a branch above the hollow looking at them.

"I'm your new leader!" he said putting a hand on his chest. They all laughed except Paul who remarked that Alice had to get back.

"It's the first time you have worried about it," said Alice.

Benjamin could see the break in the trees and through it the fields sloping towards the distant houses and the silver river that slid under the town bridge.

He put the bag deep in the hollow as Lord Augustus had advised him to do, on a bed of dry seed shells and acorns that cracked and smelled as he trod about on them.

Minutes later they were standing at the edge of the wood. Fields of corn spread down to the hedges and beyond them were more fields, smaller in the distance. Far away, the town shimmered in the afternoon mists.

Alice started to run. Then they all followed, seized with a wild feeling as they turned into the wind. Several times they stumbled on the rough ground.

Alice was behind them now. She was trying to keep up with them, through the corn field with the red poppies. She stopped. Her nose ached. She called out: "Hey! How can I keep up with you when I'm carrying Pig?"

Once Yanina stopped quite still. She let the others go ahead. Paul was looking into the small piece of coppice by the hedge where the farmer had been standing in the wild garlic. Yanina raised her arms and waved, keeping an eye on the others in case they turned and looked. It is possible, she thought, that aunt is looking through Uncle Stephen's telescope, although it is unlikely.

Then they crossed Mabbs' field where the white horse jogged its head trying to keep away a cloud of flies, although not seeming to be impatient about it. Alice was the first to leave. She barely said goodbye looking instead into the box and saying to the pig, "Poor Pig, are you all right?"

She started to climb the stairs to their room at the top. Most of the doors on the landings were bolted and looked very old and dry. She peered into one room where the bolt had dropped off. She often did this. It was full of old rags and some mattresses. Sometimes Mr Mabbs would bring more old things like that so that all the rooms were full except theirs. She thought that Mr Mabbs might be very rich owning so much property.

As she neared the door of their room, she said to herself — I will use up the jar of fish paste. We will have fish-paste sandwiches for tea!

* * *

Yanina returned by way of the brook. She was overshadowed by the tall grasses. The banks were warm and muddy and smelled sweet. In some places they were so close she could scarcely squeeze through. The brook was deep enough just before Mr Carey's garden for her to wash the mud off her shoes.

Then she saw her aunt near the strawberry bed, talking to Mr Carey. Yanina stood still, thinking of the bother the shoes would cause. Mr Carey was staking his chrysanthemums. Now he straightened up, one hand on his back. She heard him say "This morning, along the brook, I saw her." Then he was pushing his pipe tobacco down and puffing great clouds of smoke. She had often seen him do this. He had explained that because of his fingers being covered in mud it did not hurt.

What shall I do! thought Yanina, swiping at a cloud of gnats.

Her aunt, seeing the movement, turned sharply.

"Where have you been? Answer me!" she said, without giving her time to do so. "I have just told Mrs Potter I was going to look for you. Fancy the bother you have caused!"

"I have been for a walk," said Yanina, climbing up the bank.

"And look at your shoes!"

As they walked up the garden her aunt said: "Take your shoes off when you get inside. Mrs Potter won't want your mess after she's made everywhere clean."

As they walked into the kitchen her aunt began to say to Mrs Potter who was standing by the table, "I've found . . ."

Then she gazed at her without saying any more. Mrs Potter's mouth had opened in surprise. One hand was holding a joint of ham which should have been in the pantry. In her other hand she held a carving knife. There were several slices of ham in a brown paper bag on the table.

After Mrs Potter had gone and her aunt was making sandwiches for tea, Yanina said "She should not take our ham should she? She has no right to!"

Yanina had not even asked her how her leg was.

Her aunt was looking at her out of the corner of her eyes. Up to now she had always sided with Mrs Potter!

It was the way her aunt put the sandwiches firmly in front of her saying "There!" that helped Yanina decide that in spite of her muddy shoes, which were now drying beside the kitchen range, she was being welcomed back home.

Next morning she woke up earlier than usual and went into the kitchen to make tea. On the sideboard in its place was Uncle Stephen's telescope. She looked at it closely. She was sure it had not been moved. It could do with a clean! Then she took the tea up waxy-smelling stairs. As she opened the door her aunt called out sharply, "What is it? What is the matter?"

"I have brought you a cup of tea," said Yanina.

She watched Yanina carefully as she placed the pot on her bedside table.

"I think perhaps you had better pour it," said Yanina.

After she had gone, her aunt rested there for several minutes staring into the room. Then she sat up, patted the pillows and poured herself a cup of tea.

Yanina had taken Uncle Stephen's telescope from the dresser. Her aunt had gone to the shops so she was able to experiment in the way she looked at things. Standing by the back door she focused on Mr Carey's garden and found him in his shed. She quickly moved the telescope in case he should look up and think her rude. There were circles of light and colours that should not have been there. It was an old telescope.

Then she turned it to the wood on the hill, looking at it urgently, as if she expected to see Lord Augustus standing by the edge of it, nodding his approval. But for all her interest in the wood at that moment, the summer passed without Yanina making another journey to it.

* * *

Before he went to bed Benjamin cleaned and polished the van.

Mr Weekes said: "Mother, tell him he can use the steps."

"You heard what your father said!"

"It's on account of the bottom half looking stupid if it's not clean on top."

Then Benjamin cleaned the inside.

As time went by he noticed that the cheese or egg and cress sandwiches Mrs Weekes sometimes made were always eaten up and that the van came back empty. "Do you know," Benjamin heard his father say, although his mother and father were not aware of it, "I do believe the boy has brought me luck with the way he looks after the van."

He never supplied Mr Wallis again, which Benjamin thought a pity. Once on a Sunday walk, with Mr Weekes wearing his floppy velvet hat and Benjamin walking only a few paces behind them, they saw Mr Wallis. He passed them in his motor car, raising his hat courteously. Mr Weekes started to speak vigorously, looking straight ahead. But Mrs Weekes, Benjamin noticed, inclined her head nodding as much as the circumstances allowed, and gave him an altogether friendly smile.

That afternoon after lunch, Mr Weekes seemed more tired than usual. Mrs Weekes was lightly dusting the furniture and the red and green and orange ornaments with her cockerel feather duster.

Benjamin was holding his hand to his mouth, about to sneeze.

"Don't disturb your father!" Mrs Weekes whispered.

Instead of going to the top of the house to Mr Yates he went to their small back garden.

Then Mrs Weekes came out saying: "Your poor father is so tired. And he's much too tired to look after your pigeon now that you've gone off it."

"But I've taken him food!" said Benjamin.

"There's its cleaning out," said Mrs Weekes firmly, "so all in all I've arranged for it to be collected."

Benjamin said "But Mr Yates!"

Some nights Benjamin would wake up shouting. They were strange dark dreams, fed by a glut of fancies during the day. Once he dreamed of the autumn with the leaves falling as if he really knew in his sleep what was happening. He dreamed a bird was flying over the autumn gardens, with their red berries and rickety yellow leaves.

One day, long after Mr Yates had gone he went up to the empty pigeon loft. The old lady was sitting with her head in her hands by the teapot. There was no bacon smell but a smell of bonfire smoke from the other gardens. The marbles were on the shelf. He put them in his pocket, looking down uncertainly at the old lady's small patch of lawn as if undecided what to do. Then he cried out suddenly, "Oh Mr Yates! Mr Yates!"

It could have been this visit to the loft which caused him to dream again that night. But Benjamin thought it was more likely to be the muffins eaten before going to bed, a thing Mrs Weekes would not normally have allowed.

Mrs Weekes had begun: "Your father has brought you home some muffins seeing that . . ." but Mr Weekes interrupted. "I can tell the lad directly," he said. "That they are liked by you and deserved." As if at a loss to know how to go on, he added only "Deserved, that is."

Whether it was the muffins or not he dreamed a clear and disturbing dream that night. Either he was smaller or Mr Yates was bigger, otherwise the position he found himself in would have been impossible. He had his arm around Mr Yates' neck. Lord Augustus was telling him to come away.

Next morning Benjamin climbed up to the loft. He did not open the door leading to it. Instead he turned a large rusty key. First he tried with one hand, then both. He took the key and climbed on to a tea chest, so that he could touch the roof tiles. He shut his eyes; feeling the tiles with his hands; not opening his eyes so that he would not know exactly where he had hidden it. He pressed the key under one of the tiles.

This way he could not find it again easily and the door could stay shut always unless there was a very good reason to open it.

* * *

Benjamin had not been to the woods again that summer, although he had often thought about it, and about Lord Augustus in particular.

But, thought Benjamin, he probably was just an old tramp and is not there anymore.

When Alice called and stood at the front door the curiosity of going to the woods again grew upon him.

"What about them?" Alice jerked her head towards the kitchen. "Did they mind the last time?"

"They didn't know," said Benjamin. "They didn't even notice I'd been away most of the day."

"Well, ask them!"

She was so different to other children. She stood uncertainly, seemingly at an angle, her eyes dancing about looking at the position of things around her. It was as if she was always ready to run.

Benjamin did not want to ask her inside, because he knew his mother would not like it.

"The leaves are coming off and we can go chestnutting," Alice was saying.

"Have you asked Paul: is he coming?"

"I asked him," said Alice, biting her lip, "and I was told by the people to go away and not go there anymore, except by the back door for odds and ends. His father said I'd be welcome doing that, but not for his son. That's what he said."

"Paul has changed," Benjamin said. Then "Look there's no need for messages and that sort of thing. Ask Yanina if she wants to come. We won't bother with Paul I don't think."

"Do you want to come out now with me?" There's a cart in Mr Mabbs' yard. It has old leather reins still and the buckles are there. You can sit in it."

"No. I must go in."

But Alice stood there, looking in her quick way into the passage.

"You must go away," Benjamin said.

So the three went to the woods again and gathered chestnuts from the trees that grew on the edge.

Benjamin called out: "Look I've found the hollow tree and the tools are there still."

They shared out the chestnuts sitting in a hazel shelter which Benjamin had built.

Yanina said: "I would like to take an extra bag for Mrs Potter."

"Why?" asked Alice.

Yanina told them about the ham.

Alice said: "Take another bag."

It happened to be Mrs Potter's day and when Yanina returned she called out to her aunt, "I'm back!".

"So I see."

"We collected some chestnuts. May I put them on the stove?"

"Prick them first."

Yanina put the second bag on the table and said awkwardly, "Mrs Potter's I thought."

But when later she gave them to her, there was no twinkle in her eyes. She realized then, that sometimes things could never be the same again. She wondered also about the wood: whether they would ever find the path again. For they had searched by the hollow tree. They had looked for the path. Going back from the edge of the wood the gooseberry bushes would have been on the left. But there was nothing there.

12

The Man from the Ministry

BUT ALICE OFTEN WENT TO THE WOODS, alone, in spite of the approaching winter. Once she found a clump of willow coppice that was just right for peg making. She told Wilfred about it, but he did not seem interested.

"It is too far to walk," he said, "my legs are not like they were."

Alice wanted to make pegs by herself one day so she walked to the wood to look for more willow. Wilfred did not mind as long as she was back in time for tea. She passed tresses of red berries in the hedges. The hedge twigs were grey and shiny. She talked to herself about the animal signs. She saw a raven perched on a leaning post. Because she spoke to herself she did not miss having Wilfred's company.

Once going to the woods, she passed by the farmer they had met standing in the patch of wild garlic. He was layering a hedge with his billhook. She stood silently gazing at him. He looked cold and he had a red spot on his chin.

Alice said "Good morning."

"Hello Missy," he replied.

She always went the same way to the woods. Out of Mr Mabbs' yard and past the rows of cottages. The doors were shut because of the wintry weather. Alice would stand on the pavement and try to remember the old ladies, in particular the one who had been cooking dumplings or something steamy like that, with her back half turned.

The January rains ceased and the brook water became clear to look at again. Now some of the cottage doors were left open and Alice could peer in to them on the way to the woods. Further on she would pass the same yellow weed field where Benjamin had apologized about Paul and had come back to walk with her and Pig.

She now knew every place where the peg willow grew. But she had not seen the path. She mentioned it to Wilfred. He remembered no such thing. Also, she spoke to him once about Lord Augustus.

Alice asked herself: If I thought I heard a flute, then how also did I hear Pig whistling and the squeaky bats in spite of it?

The older trees had groaned and creaked in the winter wind and some had split with the weight of ice on their branches. Then the ice and snow melted and the water gushed away from the dams of sticks and moss; a sight which had earlier made Alice quiver with cold.

She had gone there several times in the hard weather, sheltering in Benjamin's hut. She laced dried ferns in between the hazel sticks. She built a small fire outside taking great care to position it so that sparks did not set it alight. She heated water and cocoa in a pot which she carried with her. She did not bring Pig on these winter journeys.

She wondered about the others. She thought of them playing snakes and ladders; the flames from their coal fires flickering and making the room shadows leap.

Benjamin and Yanina went to the woods the same way; past the field of yellow flowers, some of them bent low with the weight of congregating beetles. They barely noticed the blood red poppies in the field. It was their first journey since collecting chestnuts in the autumn past.

Sitting in the shelter, Yanina said: "I saw Alice going to people's front doors with pegs."

"So have I," said Benjamin.

"She's been here, in the shelter."

"There's no reason why she can't use it!"

"I didn't say she could not," Yanina replied, adding "It is not exactly that I don't want Alice with us. She has changed."

"It is awkward, that's all," said Benjamin. "I like Alice but my parents don't like her calling."

"She moves from foot to foot when she's standing at the door and my aunt says it's the sort of thing you'd expect Mrs Potter to do."

Benjamin and Yanina went to the woods again. They searched for but could not find the broken down old buildings where they had seen Lord Augustus.

Brambles and ferns and fallen trees made exploring difficult.

But they did not go to the woods again with Alice.

Alice did not mind the brambles and the thick shadowy places of the woods. She knew about different things: the smells of mushrooms and moss and the existence of deep ravines laced over with crackly sticks and ferns. She often looked for the path; feeling it was better to do it alone, although she liked the others, except Paul.

Sometimes she saw a raven and wondered if it was the same old raven with its black eyes like the colour of the middle of a broken field-flint.

Once, in fact, she felt very strange at the head of a way into the woods. She stumbled into the sea of green leaves only to be thrown to the ground by a tree stump. "Next time," Alice said, rubbing her knee, "I will bring Pig with me. Then I will not be alone."

* * *

Paul did not worry about Alice. He now went to a boarding school and had new friends. He had a pinewood tuck box and at least one dozen white shirts.

Once she had knocked on the back door for some left-overs, and Paul was in the kitchen and the maid and butler were laughing at one of his jokes.

Paul did not talk directly to Alice.

"Oh give her some more!" he said, pointing at a leg of lamb. "More! More! More!"

"The master . . ." said the butler uncertainly.

Paul looked at him steadily. The maid had stopped laughing.

"That will be all right," said Paul, " if you will do as I say."
Alice said "I don't mind. It will do."

Paul turned to look at her. Two red patches appeared on her
cheeks. She grabbed the package, feeling the warmth of the
meat through the greaseproof paper. As she ran home, she
cried out aloud, several times "I will never go there! Never
again! Never!"

*   *   *

As the summer wore on she thought about sending messages.

She was sitting in the old cart in Mabbs' yard. The half-
rotten leather reins had finally broken. "I will send a message
in a bottle down the brook to Yanina." Finally she did. The
water was low in the brook. For days it stayed in one place,
and when the bottle finally moved past Mr Carey's garden
Yanina had her back turned. In any case, Alice reasoned,
Yanina could not have known it was there.

She had found a case of empty green medicine bottles
complete with corks. She put several in the brook but never
one for Paul and thought of different tasks for both of them.
But she really knew that the messages would not be received,
and so tired of it.

The summer ended abruptly. The chestnuts fell to the
ground but this time were left ungathered. Alice was too
involved in making pegs to even think about them. She had
determined never again to go to the Mayor's kitchen. Wilfred
had asked her to, saying that the uphill walk made him feel
giddy. But she found one excuse after the other. It was for this
reason that she had learned how to make pegs, although she
was slow with it, so that this could buy their food.

Once Yanina had walked by her. Alice was not certain but
thought it likely that Yanina had meant to do it.

She had been standing by the front door of one of the
cottages on the edge of the town. The lady who made dumplings usually bought a few pegs from her and sometimes gave
her an extra penny. This time, the lady had shaken her head.
When Alice turned again, Yanina had gone.

But Benjamin was always polite and friendly. He had called
after her in the middle of the town, "I heard your father is not

very well. I haven't seen him about."

"He stays at home."

"Oh well I hope he gets better soon."

Alice thought then about asking him to come and sit in the old cart in Mabbs' yard. Although the reins had fallen apart, she had cut a long willow stick for the use of the driver. But she did not ask him and after a while they parted.

*   *   *

Even the men's draper, thinking in the depths of his shop, with the fancy ties and socks, missed Wilfred. He had often felt annoyed with him, as he had seen him sit down in the shop front with his flute; raising his hat to the motor cars.

Wilfred could watch for the powdery blue butterflies circling in the warm air; or note the sly looks of people as they went by his upturned hat, and appear to be entertained by it all in a way the draper could not understand.

Wilfred had seemed to have nothing else to do. But now the draper missed him and sent some yellow socks.

The preacher's wife and other people left more than the usual number of parcels at the bottom of the stairs. Sometimes they were marked 'For Wilfred' or just 'Wilfred' or for 'Wilfred and Alice'. Even the butcher had given them some meat which he said he did not want and he had walked upstairs with it. The lady who made dumplings had given Alice a whole seed cake.

But still Alice made pegs. The skin on her hands was rough where she gripped the wood. She cut the pegs to length and tacked the strips of tin around one end. Wilfred shaped most of them, as he sat in his chair. "Time will come Alice when you must do this yourself, although there's no need these days with more than enough in the cupboard."

But, Alice thought furiously, I want to make pegs. There is a need for making pegs. She said: "We're the only people to get things for nothing."

Alice did not say any more because Wilfred looked so grey in his chair.

She had less time to look for the woodland path. She often thought about it, as she rested on her mattress next to Pig.

She brought home bundles of willow, which she cut with great care, now that the leaf was off. Before the real winter set in she had a good supply of wood.

When she returned from one of her peg selling journeys round the town, she saw only Wilfred's empty chair. There was a message on the table which read 'gone wooding'. That meant cutting peg wood.

At first Alice was pleased that he had felt well enough to leave the room. But, she thought, he must have realized that they had more than enough wood for their needs! She noticed that the jar of goose fat had been moved to another shelf as if he had picked it up and looked at it. Whenever he did that, although it was not often, his cheeks would look pinched and Alice always knew very well that it would be no good at all to talk to him about anything for a while.

He did not turn up for tea.

The elder bushes in Mabbs' yard started to look black against a deeply coloured sunset. By this time she was afraid. Alice shivered, half listening to the crickets chirruping in the warm evening air.

She knew Benjamin would help her. But Mrs Weekes did not like her on the doorstep! She did not want to bother Yanina and she had vowed never again to go to the Mayor's house.

First of all she filled a box with straw and fixed a strap to it. Then she put Pig in it and started walking towards the outskirts of the town, on her way to the woods. The stars had started to glint. First the evening star then the stars on the edge of the world. Real owls fled from a garden screeching wildly.

In vain Alice tried to feel again the courage of that first night under the pines in their back garden, with her long, cut-out cardboard scimitar!

As she approached the door of the lady who made dumplings, she paused. Then she knocked. She had lost any sense about what was the right and polite thing to do. She rattled away at the knocker without stopping. Before the door opened, another down the street opened and then another. The dumpling-making lady took one look at Alice and pulled her in.

Sitting in a chair, wrapped in a blanket, although the weather was not cold, Alice told her of her fears.

The lady said she would call her husband, which she did. He was a small man in a faded pink shirt. For a time they spoke together, now and then glancing at Alice.

"Well my dear," said the lady, "Mr Pardoe will go out directly and send for the authorities who will no doubt make a search."

"I can go with them!"

"Small girls will hinder, not help. Now my dear, you can rest where you are." Then turning to her husband she added "Get some bedding from the cupboard and an apple for her pig."

In the morning there seemed to be more birdsong in the woods than usual. The air was traced with woodsmoke drifting across from a fire of hedge cuttings.

They had not known where to look. Their lanterns had revealed nothing and there had been no answer to their calls. But now with the sun well risen the searchers seemed guided to the place. Webs glistened, the wild red berries glowed with an unearthly light and in such profusion that at least one searcher stopped to rub his eyes.

Then the blackbirds and the pigeons had flown off. A woodcock zig-zagged through the coppice. The white tails of rabbits showed for a moment in the deep parts of the wood where there was little sun. As they reached a clearing an utter silence fell.

They had found Wilfred.

*   *   *

The lady who made dumplings whose name was Mrs Pardoe, although Alice did not think of her as that, said to Alice that she could not go back to her room until things had been sorted out. But when she was in the larder, at the same time as Mr Pardoe was digging potatoes in the garden, Alice left with Pig, running down the street as hard as she could. When she reached her room she put on the kettle and made tea. Then she locked the door and held Pig on her lap. How long she sat there she did not know. She had put all their possessions on the pine table.

These were several old toys and faded pictures. There was the picture of Wilfred and his bride and her family standing on the chapel steps after their marriage, squinting in the sunlight. She did not include food in this display of their possessions, except the jar of goose fat which she supposed could be eaten in an emergency, although it must now taste very old.

Then she put the pig on the table as well and thought: I wonder how long Pig will last? Pigs do not have a long life!

Then her thoughts scattered as there was a persistent knocking on the door.

"Please open up!" It was a man's voice.

Alice kept quiet.

In a kindly tone the man said: "If you are there please open the door. Otherwise I will have to break it in to get in. It don't help."

"There is a lady," he said patiently, "who is enquiring after you. Mrs Pardoe."

"Dumplings," said Alice, after letting him in.

"I beg your pardon?"

"I watched her make dumplings at the pot."

"I see," he said. "But she is too old for us. We don't have middle-aged people keeping children like that."

"Why not?" asked Alice.

"It would be all right for visits. You know the sort of thing. I'm sure she makes a very nice cake. But unless you have a relative, which I understand you have not, then you must go into care."

"Is that very bad?" asked Alice, adding "I had a mother."

"Exactly. But where is she?"

"Who are you?" Alice asked with as much politeness as she could muster.

"I am from the Ministry," he said. Then he noticed one of Wilfred's silver painted boots. He changed the subject to make her at ease: "Surely that boot has been painted?"

"He painted all his boots silver," said Alice. "There's a tin of it on the table."

"It don't seem a natural thing to do," he said coughing.

"Now my dear, I have a bag for you to put some things in."

Alice reached for the goose fat.

"We wouldn't like that."

"I will run," said Alice, surprised at her spirit.

"Well, then, I expect you could ask the Matron."

But Alice agreed to leave the silver paint. She took Pig with her.

On the staircase they met Mrs Pardoe. She was breathing heavily with the exertion of the climb. She was wearing a hat trimmed with fur. Alice had never seen her look like this before. She was close to her; able to smell the wardroby smell of her clothes.

"You wait at the bottom of the staircase," said the man from the Ministry, "and stay there. Don't forget I'm carrying the bag with the goose fat!"

Later he joined her and said "Come along my dear" and Mrs Pardoe had smiled rather shakily saying: "You will be allowed to visit me if you wish."

"But not too frequent," the man from the Ministry said, adding to Mrs Pardoe "It's disturbing, you understand me? It don't do good."

13

Journey with a Pram

FOR A YEAR OR MORE ALICE DID NOT GROW. It was as if the sight every evening of the enamel jug with the thin, bitter cocoa, or being in the dormitory with the other children, had shocked her into staying exactly as she was.

Then suddenly she grew. Her cheekbones stood out more than ever; her wide mouth set firm as she ignored the banter. When she talked she still shifted from foot to foot, glancing to the side and beyond as she spoke.

She had pinned the family photograph, as she called it, on the wall behind her bed. They would say Who is it? Why aren't you living with them? Are they gypsies? You're a gypsy!

There was one girl who was thinner than Alice and who listened seriously to what Alice had to say about the photograph.

"For a start," said Alice, "I'm here because my parents have gone abroad."

"Are they dead?"

"They may be," Alice said, "but if they are it will be abroad. The sun was shining into people's faces when the picture was took. But my mother as you see was a pretty person. She could have been on the stage."

The other children heard of it and the photograph was pulled off the wall and Alice had taken the pegging knife from under her mattress where she had hidden it and held it tightly in her hand, the colour draining from her fingers, shouting: "Give it back! Give!"

She had no idea of moving with the knife: of going to a child and using the knife. It felt much like holding the cardboard scimitar because she was afraid. Only this was a real knife and the governors said she ought to be sent away but that this was more or less the last place for a girl to be in.

The children tried to take the bottle of goose fat. But she looked so white and strange they backed away.

She was gradually left alone.

Alice had once seen a tame fox at the back of some tents in a fair, chained to a stake. A lady was boiling a can of water over a wood fire, for tea. All the noise of the fair was on the other side of the tents. The lady had said nothing but had glanced at Alice occasionally. The fox was neither friendly nor hostile. Alice could get close. It sometimes flicked its ear. An upside-down picture of the tents was in the fox's eyes.

They had backed away from Alice. She was left alone at last, like an animal that had been brought in from the wild, and forgotten.

She was allowed to visit Mrs Pardoe at Christmas and for a week during the summer.

Mrs Pardoe's house was small, although Mr Pardoe fitted into it naturally, wherever he was.

When Mrs Pardoe was cooking meat or steaming puddings and those sort of things, the brown walls in the passageway were very soon covered with the condensing steam. Often cake smells rose up the steep staircase and into the top bedroom with the wallpaper of pink roses.

So because there was no room Alice stayed in the garden shed. She honestly preferred this, in spite of the onion sets in boxes and the carrot and parsnip seed hanging in muslin bags from the beams to keep them out of the reach of mice. Mr Pardoe also kept bunches of orange-coloured chinese lantern flowers there until they were dry and ready to go indoors to decorate the tiny front room. In spite of all this Alice looked upon the shed as her home.

One Christmas Mr and Mrs Pardoe gave her a gilt frame for her family photograph. She put it on the wall over her bed next to the onions and did not take it back with her to the Home. Mr Pardoe had built a small stove with a pipe that went through the roof, so it was rarely cold in winter. If it was, then it only made Alice think back happily to some of the times when she and Wilfred had been obliged to stay out in the open or sleep in farm buildings, with the owners not knowing anything about it. She had been very cold on most of these occasions.

Sometimes Alice would run away from the Home. She would not go to Mrs Pardoe's because that was always the first place where the officials called. Mrs Pardoe said: "Alice, you must not do it, child. D'you understand? It is a worry for me and Mr Pardoe especially."

Mr Pardoe said later: "The fact is, she's not ours. If she was allowed to be here more often we might make her see."

"No she's not ours," Mrs Pardoe sighed, "and never will be."

"Nor should we have expectations," said Mr Pardoe.

She usually ran away in the late summer, when it was easy to live rough because of the berries and nuts and warm nights. She returned after a few days and was kept away from the other children and had meals on her own for a week or two. Then as she grew older she would run away more often, always to her 'own wood' where they could not find her.

It was nearly time for her to leave.

The Secretary to the Board of Governors said: "Gentlemen, we have prepared her as much as we can for the world."

"An ungrateful hussy!"

"You can only do so much for people of this sort," said the Secretary.

Wood anemones studded the dark woodland floor. The banks and clearings were covered with primroses although Alice did not touch them. When she ran away this time no one was sent to Mrs Pardoe to search for her and another child was given her bed. She had brought her jar of goose fat with her. It was as if strangely she had known that this time there would be no place for her at the Home anymore.

She went along the winding country lanes watching the cloud shadows leap from hill to hill. She started peg making again, having bought another knife at a fair, where the music was very loud, making her ears sing. Her journeys became longer, taking her to other woods and across fields where there were none of the familiar flints, with the black heart which showed when they were broken.

A lady gave her an old pram in which she could put her possessions and pegs and the sheets to keep away the rain.

The days of the carts were over and now it was the motor cars that splashed her. No driver would look sorry about it.

Now dark and thin; if she had been gowned in a cream-coloured gown with gold slippers and just with Alice's face, people would have looked in wonder. For Alice was beautiful under the dirt. But her hair had become matted and people in the streets tended to look down as they had sometimes with Wilfred. Once in a village, pushing her pram, she passed a vicar in a new-looking, crisp white hat, but he did not raise it to her or look her way.

Although her journeys were long, Alice came back to Mrs Pardoe's for Christmas and to the wood at the top of the hill.

Then even these visits stopped.

But wherever Alice was beckoned, by the violet-covered banks or the distant sun on the fields, she always thought of the wood she had loved as a child and which in her heart she knew only as Lord Augustus' wood.

PART THREE

14

Strong Like a Lion

TWO MEN WERE STANDING in Mabbs' yard, the appearance of which had altered with the years. Seedlings blown from the pine trees in Alice's old garden had taken root next to the heaps of rusted iron. One of the men seemed infuriated with the other. He started to clamber over the old cart that Alice had once sat in.

"Of course I would clear all this rubbish but I'll not reduce my price." Saying this he fell through the rotten flooring and cursed.

The nestling blackbirds and their parents were making a great commotion. For no one had been in Mabbs' yard since Alice had gone away.

Paul's companion said: "You did very well to buy it so cheaply."

"I went to the auction. You could have gone."

"I was prevented from doing so. But no matter."

"I repeat," said Paul, "I will not reduce my price."

"What good will your yard be to you by itself?"

"Since you want to build houses in Mabbs' field, what good will your field be to you by itself?"

"I will have to find a way."

"There is no other way! There can be no road to and from your houses except through the yard."

"Look my dear chap, if we help each other, we can both be rich." He smiled and rested a hand on Paul's shoulder.

Paul fidgeted with his neatly cut blond moustache. It gleamed with the scented oil he had combed into it. His eyes had not altered and he still stared at people. He stared now.

His companion became uneasy. Then he shrugged his shoulders and walked away, past where the old chicken hut used to be, and on to the road. He will pay my price, Paul thought, and if he doesn't, then I paid so little for the yard, I will not mind if I never see my money back again.

Mabbs' yard did not remind Paul of Alice or Yanina, or the leafy smells in the wood on the hill or the corn field and the poppies. He thought of Benjamin, and that was because he worked in the bank as a clerk. He wondered how Benjamin would feel about him if he became one of the bank's richest customers. He stood awhile before returning to his father's house; dreaming of the sound of tea cups clattering and people talking in the way they do at garden parties. He would buy an old mansion away from the town, with gardens kept by a gardener and an under-gardener. He would have a car with green leather seats; oil paintings of himself and his father and his wife although he had not met her yet. And goldfish! Fat yellow fish and pale pink fish streaked with black, and marigold-coloured fish. Paul said to himself: 'For all these pleasures, all I have to do is wait!'

On his way home he sauntered along streets once familiar to Wilfred. Since Paul had been on the town council there had been changes. For example, the old draper's shop entrance, which had been Wilfred's favourite resting place was now cleaned and painted and was an ironmongery. No more beetles and cracked paint or woodlice or drapers who could not pay the rates!

He called at a small general store.

"A pound of walnuts, if you please."

"Shelled or unshelled?"

"Unshelled will do very well," he said with a smile.

Paul looked at his father's hands turning white at the knuckles as he strove to break the shells. He was still fat and wore deep green and blue waistcoats and sometimes a canary yellow waistcoat. But his hair was grey and his hands shook. He thought contemptuously: He is old and weak. He has no more strength in his hand than a sick girl's.

"Go away," his father said. "Do you know," he went on, turning to his wife, "our dog smells worse than ever!"

"Of dog, my dear."

"Well, hardly of anything else. I will not have it when I eat. Go away I say!"

For no reason that Paul could think of, he shivered.

He would tell them now, Paul decided. It would be amusing to watch his father, who was always saying I did this and I did that, when I was Mayor. His mother was resting on the sofa, her head on a velvet cushion. Her lids were shut to ward off the sight of the ex-Mayor eating the nuts and spilling the shells on the carpet, a habit which she had always found detestable. Her lids were frail and veined and weak-looking like poppy petals. They quivered only slightly when Paul said: "Of course you know don't you that I'm putting in for Mayor?"

Well I might have known, his father thought.

And he had considered for a minute, struggling to break a shell; his fat hands trembling and changing colour: "If you are standing for Mayor, then this transaction of yours, to do with Mabbs' yard isn't it? Well, make money discreetly. People envy wealth. They will only vote for you if they like you."

"People admire success above all else," said Paul. He sighed and added "and I am rather successful!"

In the autumn he was elected Mayor. As the leaves started to fall off the elder bushes, the taking away of the scrap iron had started. "If you take away all the rubbish and clear the site, I will pay your price. But first the clearing must be done."

Paul had won! To be strong like a lion!

He reflected that even as a boy he had been a leader.

He even remembered the feeling of triumph, it was not joy, as he had leapt over and over the brook shouting, so that old Mabbs' horse had looked, then shaken its head before bending to the grass again.

It was strange, Paul decided, the things that were remembered.

It rained steadily. So work shifted to the demolition of Mabbs' building. The men wore helmets and steel tipped boots. They had flasks of hot tea and ate bread and cheese for their dinner. One of them had a dirty bandage on his finger.

There was no question of tapping out nails and straightening them as Mr Carey had done with some of the nails from his seed boxes, putting them in jars labelled 'one inch nails', 'half inch nails', and 'mixed nails'. They started at the top. They wrenched the cupboard off the wall; the cupboard in which Wilfred had kept his food and personal things like the goose fat and silver paint. It all went through the window which of course had been smashed out to make it possible.

Occasionally the ground shook and the blackbirds fled in dismay from the bushes.

15

Benjamin and Yanina

IN THE EVENINGS Benjamin would sit quietly at home reading. But at the bank he was a different person. At first his mother made him sandwiches, as she had done for Mr Weekes. Then as Benjamin's position at the bank improved, he had lunch in the back room of the cake shop.

"Seeing that he keeps himself to himself, it's surprising that he's got on so well; understanding people and having a way with them."

Mr Weekes answered: "He gets it from me."

"I dare say you're right dear," said Mrs Weekes gently.

Benjamin dealt with most queries admirably, occasionally referring a matter to the chief clerk or to the manager.

Every Christmas, Mrs Pardoe would call at the bank, to cash a small cheque from a relative in the north. She would dress up specially, wearing her old fur-trimmed hat; taking greater care than usual to nod at acquaintances. Benjamin would ask: "Is Alice staying with you this Christmas?" and they would talk for a while: always, it seemed to Mrs Pardoe's surprise afterwards, about herself or Mr Pardoe. Last year she had brought him a quarter slice of seed cake. She would say to Mr Pardoe: "Such a nice young man! He's always so attentive. A real gentleman."

As Christmas approached Benjamin wondered, Should I ask about Alice? It will worry her I daresay to think about it. For last Christmas she had not seen Alice, and he had heard that last summer Alice had still not been seen.

Mr Wallis was another customer. He had sold his business. He was still known as Bony Wallis or Old Bony. Certainly he would crack his hands at least once as he waited to be served by his favourite cashier at the bank.

Whenever Benjamin saw him, he would do something like count money or refer to a ledger, or say, 'Just a minute Mr Wallis', as he talked to a junior clerk about a matter which it seemed had suddenly occurred to him. It was not to keep Mr Wallis waiting; it was, if Benjamin had known it, so that he could compose himself. For once Mr Wallis had talked about the table, as he waited for his money to be counted: "I remember it clearly! Your poor father! Is he well by the way?"

"He is well thank you."

"Such beauty!" Mr Wallis had a sudden spasm of bone cracking. "It had something to do with the sun coming in. Streaming in. That's what it was; the colours of the marbles and the beauty of the table. You see it was so straightforward."

Benjamin had stopped counting.

Mr Wallis was saying quietly, almost to himself: "So many people, you understand, all manner of people do not use their gifts."

Mr Wallis' money was stacked in a small pile ready for re-counting. Benjamin said, clearing his throat, "Will a pound's worth of silver be all right Mr Wallis?"

By his hand was the wet sponge he used when counting notes. He had cut it to shape and put it in an old sugar dish. The middle of the sponge was worn where his finger had pressed and pressed and pressed.

One day after that incident Mr Wallis had thought: He is a very correct young man. Not a bit like his father. Keeps a distance between people; that's it! Not a bad thing at all.

The familiar sounds of Mrs Weekes clearing away the Sunday dinner had lulled Mr Weekes to sleep. She no longer pottered about the house dusting with her cockerel feather duster, saying to Benjamin "Don't disturb your father!"

In fact Mr Weekes now slept so deeply, puffing and twitching, that Mrs Weekes had, as she put it, a business getting him to come to; holding a cup of tea by his nose and assuring him that everything was all right.

Now Mrs Weekes said without bothering to go into the

kitchen: "Your father wants another interest."

Benjamin put down his book: "I thought the tables were still selling?"

"Oh yes, but he is not so active, is he? As I said he wants another interest, not just work. He's taking things a bit easy as a man of his age should."

"There's the garden."

"He doesn't like it. He sees no point in any of it. That's what he says."

"Well I cannot think . . ." said Benjamin.

"I *have* thought," said Mrs Weekes. "And I wanted to tell you about it, since you might even help him with some of the things that have to be done."

"What do you mean?"

"Like clearing out and things like that. Pigeons!"

Benjamin closed his book and shut his eyes.

"I was looking for the loft key, but I couldn't find it. Do you know where it is? *Benjamin!*"

"I don't know where it is," said Benjamin slowly.

"Don't worry," Mrs Weekes said, "I'll have another look. It's in a drawer I suppose." Then she looked at Mr Weekes, "I'll disturb him with his cup of tea in a while."

She looked for it again during the week. She said to Benjamin, "Perhaps you threw it away." After that she seemed to forget about it.

But for weeks afterwards Benjamin found himself thinking about the key under the tiles. He could even see it in his mind's eye. He had turned it using both hands!

Once in the bank he was thinking so deeply about the loft and the key wedged under the tile and the smell of bacon long ago that at first he did not see the new Mayor standing in front of him, stroking his blonde moustache, waiting for Benjamin to say "Good morning!"

"Good morning!" said Benjamin.

"Good morning, Weekes!"

There was little conversation between them beyond How would you like the notes? and Fives would do very well or Ones would do very well.

Once Paul had said "How's your father?"

Benjamin had stopped counting and made a note on a scrap

of paper answering "He is keeping well thank you. How is yours?"

He had looked steadily at Paul, waiting for an answer. Eventually Paul had to look away. He started to finger his moustache.

Afterwards a junior clerk had said "Do you know what I thought, Mr Weekes? I think he could open a can of sardines with the way he stares."

Benjamin dealt with Paul efficiently and quickly. He never made a mistake in counting. He pounded the sponge in the manner of a postmaster or a government inspector of some kind. With other customers he did not seem to be like that. In fact with people like Mrs Pardoe his finger would gently rest on the sponge as they passed the time of day. He did not allow himself to be intimidated by Paul. The sponge helped. The tall windows, the polished mahogany counters were a source of strength.

If sometimes he felt overwhelmed, he would forcibly think back to Lord Augustus, counting the notes carefully at the same time, pounding the sponge two even three times which was quite unnecessary.

He would remember Paul in the dark building and Yanina with a candle in her hand, asking Paul: "You're not afraid are you?"

Paul in his turn had to admit that Benjamin made a good cashier. Correct and helpful without being familiar and taking advantage of their childhood acquaintanceship. Weekes might even be Manager one day. He could be useful to me, he thought.

When Yanina called, Benjamin felt like a new employee, imagining himself noticeable in his suit and longing for a break in the back-room with egg and cress sandwiches. He did not behave like a highly respected cashier: the person Mrs Pardoe dressed up for: the son Mr Weekes was proud of, saying to acquaintances 'That's my boy!'

Yanina's black hair was still in long plaits, which she wound round her head. Her complexion was pale, almost creamy and her eyes had become a deeper blue. When she smiled she seemed to do so almost meditatively.

But when she called at the bank she did not smile at Benjamin because it seemed to confuse him. She regularly withdrew the interest on Uncle Stephen's shares; her aunt being unable to do so because of illness. Often, it seemed quite unnecessarily, she called merely to ask Benjamin how the shares were.

Benjamin would at times succeed in a pretence of feeling indifferent. As he smelled her scent, disturbing as it was, he would think, The same old stuff, lavender! How unoriginal! Then he would ask: "Would you like it in ones?"

They might talk. He would often have to count the money twice. Once Benjamin swept his finger to the sponge in such an erratic way that he knocked it off the counter. The junior clerk, who was quick to notice anything, picked it up and handed it to Benjamin with a smile.

Lately in the street, he would quicken his pace if he saw Yanina, detesting the impression which he felt he was creating with his idiocy.

Once in the middle of eating his soup in the back of the cake shop he had put his spoon down, staring in front of him as he inwardly raged. Why on earth am I like this? What can she possibly think?

"Is everything all right, Mr Weekes?" the girl who waited at the tables inquired.

"Oh yes. Oh yes. Yes, thank you!"

When he passed her in the street, Yanina merely bit her lip gently, as if puzzling to herself. In spite of the mistakes he made, she called even more frequently so that in all honesty the subject of Uncle Stephen's shares was quite exhausted.

16

Alice's Return

MR PARDOE LIKED HIS DAHLIAS. He would often pause by them, imprisoned in a cone of garden sounds and smells. In the early winter he would carefully lift them from the soil and spread them out on the pantry floor under the shelf. This was bending under the weight of Mrs Pardoe's jams and chutneys and salted beans.

"Pardoe," she said good humouredly, for she always called him rather curiously by his surname when feeling affectionate.

"Pardoe dear, you must prop that shelf in the middle. I've told you enough."

The dahlias had been moved in from the garden, all neatly laid out on newspaper and sprinkled with soil on the floor under the shelf.

"Also, I need the floor space where the dahlias are for pots and pans."

"Then we will have to use the garden shed. I think it's time, don't you, to use the shed again?"

"Yes," said Mrs Pardoe after a pause, "I'm afraid it is."

"For garden things I mean."

"Yes, I know."

Mr Pardoe put a sheet of corrugated iron over the bare mattress and spread the dahlias on it.

"But one thing," said Mrs Pardoe. "The photograph stays where it is. Just in case."

"If she was coming for this Christmas she would have been here by now."

"Yes, but there's always next summer."

Mr Pardoe plaited his onions into long bunches. He hung one lot of onions on the nail which also supported Alice's photograph. Mrs Pardoe never went to the garden shed because it made her think and worry over Alice. Also when she passed Mabbs' yard on the way to the shops, she turned away from the sight of the demolition work.

The building was nearly down. The rooms on the ground floor had been filled with old mattresses. One of the workmen said: "Mabbs must have been a funny old gaffer to keep on to things like that."

People in the town were talking about Mabbs' yard. It was said that the new Mayor was forcing a ridiculous price for it. Because Christmas was near Paul's father had treated himself to some Algerian dates. As he munched them he said: "Paul, people are saying that an older Mayor would have been careful not to make money so fast and in such a manner. You will allow me to be right?"

But Paul ignored him and said: "Shall I ring for a bowl of water and a towel?"

His father was wiping his hands on his waistcoat. They trembled slightly as he did so. "You will allow me?" his father said again.

But Paul still appeared to ignore him. Now he stood by a window which overlooked the garden. Starlings in their hundreds were massing in the bare tree branches. He had just thought of an idea. It would not cost a great deal of money. In any case he could afford it: And it will bring me back into favour with the people of the town, he thought.

Paul managed the town's affairs well. If there was not enough money to clean the streets, or to cut the cow parsley on the road verges and so on, then the rates had to be increased! If, like the draper who used to sit by the ties and socks, people could not pay the rates, then officials would remove them. There was no place for the weak. Because of this there were several empty shops. One of them in particular was suitable for Paul's plan, because it had a good kitchen.

Paul paid for all the tables and chairs and some of the groceries. He bought one of the first television sets that had been seen in the county. It would be open just for the Christmas period: a place where poor people could gather and be entertained and where they could eat for nothing. The townspeople had also been invited to help with serving food or providing some of it. Mrs Pardoe made three journeys with some pots of red cabbage, chutney and pickle. Mr Pardoe scratched his head and said to himself, Why then did I go to the trouble of strengthening the shelf?

Soon after that Mr and Mrs Pardoe left by train to Mrs Pardoe's relative in the north where they were to spend Christmas. Mrs Pardoe had seen Benjamin in the street and she had explained: "I will not be banking a cheque this Christmas. We are staying there instead."

Benjamin said "I hope you enjoy yourselves and have a happy Christmas", thinking, because it was an easy thing to say and you could think of something else at the same time, On no account will I ask her if she has heard from Alice!

Then after Mr and Mrs Pardoe had left, Alice turned up wheeling her old pram. She often slept rough, although mostly she stayed in hostels, during her travelling. She would willingly have slept in Mr Herbert's disused cow shed. He was the gentleman troubled with face spots, who had once frightened the children on the way to the woods, just by standing still and looking at them from the copse. She was certain of a welcome because she had always brought him some cream she made from wild herbs, which was suitable for skin disorders.

But she was seen by one of Mrs Pardoe's neighbours, who, looking at Alice, thought that she was one of the poorest and thinnest creatures she had seen for a long time. She did not recognize Alice. She directed her to the Mayor's temporary room in the High Street, where they had even started playing suitable music on a gramophone in the mornings.

So Alice went there.

She had tried Mrs Pardoe's door. Then she had gone round by the back and seen the dahlias spread out; and the onions hanging from the nail on the wall.

Like a princess, Alice walked into the place for the Christmas poor. For she created such a stir. All eyes were fixed on her;

this was exactly what they wanted! When the several lady helpers saw her they must have thought that if they wanted a poor person, then surely this was the poorest of them all!

Finally she sat down with a cup of tea and a mince pie. She thought she recognized the old man next to her. Long ago he had stared at Wilfred sprawled in the doorway of his shop.

Alice said: "Did you sell socks? We came in once."

He nodded.

"Did you know my father?"

"I couldn't say. I met lots of people. It was a nice shop."

Then the room filled with people who did not look poor at all. Alice recognized Paul who was smiling at an old lady as he offered her a mince pie.

"Once more please," said the camera man.

"Put it back," said Paul to the lady.

"Whatever for?"

"They want to take another picture. You can keep it next time."

"Come on dear," said the camera man. "Look happy! It's Christmas!" The Mayor was standing by the television set which was to be included in the photograph.

Alice's head felt as if it was floating away from her. "You're the Mayor! You *are* the Mayor aren't you?"

"Happy Christmas!" Paul beamed and went on talking to a council official.

Alice waited to make herself known.

"You know me, don't you," she said. "Excuse me," she went on, "I haven't been here for a long time."

Paul whispered something to the official who then opened the top window. "Now," said Paul turning to Alice, "you haven't been here, you said. Of course not. It only opened yesterday. Closing New Year's Day. Have some pudding?"

Someone else had offered the old lady pudding. "Got room dear?"

Once again Alice tried to speak, but Paul's back was now turned. She sat down with the pudding bowl on her lap feeling too faint to eat it. She had a peculiar drumming in her temples. Last night she had dreamed and the dream left her feeling weak like this. It was a dream of swans and a dark river. There was no moon. The lean starlight powdered things with a little light. The forms of swans loomed, disappearing, edging away on the dark water. For the tenth time that day Alice said to herself 'It is no good. I must not think about it. It is only a dream'.

Now Paul was looking at her, puzzling. He turned away.

Then Alice threw her pudding at the television set. She had scooped it up in her hand.

As she did not send the bowl as well, there was no damage.

After leaving the rooms Alice wheeled her pram around the town, keeping well away from the direction of Mabbs' yard. Her skin had the slightly waxy faded appearance of an autumn leaf. The lustre in her eyes had gone. Mrs Weekes, she thought, will not like me knocking on the door. So Alice went to Yanina's because she knew her aunt was bedridden.

She also had a present to give her, of flower-scented oil. She had cut wild flowers from the hedges, hanging them to dry. Then she had powdered them, covering it all with clear oil so that the scents infused into it. It was so pleasant to use that, during the summer, Alice had poured some into another bottle, marking it 'Yanina'. She did it with great care in the way that Wilfred had labelled the goose fat.

It was the flower oil and the fact that she had labelled it, making it in a sense already belonging to Yanina, that helped to give her the will to go back to the town for Christmas. She had not travelled from the distant woods and villages for several years because of her lack of strength.

Alice had altered so much that few people had recognized her. But as she went to Yanina's house, the butcher had seen her and recognized her. He had retired and lived a quiet life in one of the streets near Mrs Pardoe. As Alice went by he nodded. She misunderstood and fumbled in the top of her pram, thinking he wanted some clothes pegs.

But she was tired. Oh how tired she was! Although she knew they were in the bottom of the pram, she could not be bothered with it and said "I haven't any. Next time."

The butcher looked at her disappearing figure.

One or two snow flurries fell.

Finally, long after she had gone, he turned up the collar of his coat, then walked to his home.

* * *

"Happy Christmas!" Yanina said, placing the breakfast tray by her aunt's bed.

"I should have thought today, at least there would have been a change."

"You know very well that if you have anything but toast and marmalade it upsets you."

"I shan't eat it."

"Very well," said Yanina,"but I will not take it away yet." She paused by the landing on her way downstairs. The hills sloping up to the distant woods were streaked with snow. And impulsively she almost ran, bouncing her hand on the waxy banisters. Taking Uncle Stephen's telescope from the shelf she returned to the landing.

It was probably Mr Herbert burning hedge trimmings. She could also see where the powdery snow had blown off most of the fields, settling in the hedges. In spite of the patches of snow she could still pick out the white of the large unbroken flints in the top field. Looking made her eyes ache. Resting awhile she sniffed her fingers as she had done as a child, closing her eyes as she experienced the smell of brass. Thinking as she had thought then, of the calm oily seas when he had crossed out Cream of Asparagus and written in French Onion Soup.

It made her think of the ordinariness of the things you could do, before an end to something: like it had been for Uncle Stephen before he drowned: of doing ordinary idle things like looking at the hill without being able to know of what was going to happen next.

Yanina shivered as she looked at the dark wood. A column of smoke was blowing from the bonfire straight across the field. Now and then she could see a burst of orange colour from the fire as it flared up. She replaced Uncle Stephen's telescope, polishing it on her apron before doing so. The feeling of unease remained.

It's to do with Christmas, she thought. It's all right for children of course.

Later she took some mince pies to Mr and Mrs Potter. She wondered about taking some ham, but could just imagine

Mrs Potter in her shaky voice saying 'Thank you my dear. Are you sure?' and struggling with the wild memory of being seen with the carving knife in her hand.

Christmas again! thought Yanina.

"Are you all right dear?" Mrs Potter asked. "Has anything upset you?"

"Of course I'm all right," Yanina said.

"I'm so glad dear, and we're very grateful for the pies. Is your aunt as well as can be expected?"

Then in the afternoon, the children who lived in Mr Carey's old house had thrown a ball into Yanina's garden. As they crossed the brook to retrieve it, she had run down the garden shouting: "Go away from my garden, how dare you!"

She had put a plank carefully over the brook so as not to get her feet wet. She told their parents "I will not have your children in my garden!" They had apologized, then had actually said that if Yanina wished to speak to them again would she walk round the proper way and not cross their back garden over the brook! "But" their father had said politely, "please do return this time by the same way."

So Yanina had gone across the lawn again, which was still showing green in places through the powdery snow. She had to struggle to keep back tears of anger and humiliation.

Mr Carey's old potting shed was still there. The lawn sloped right down to the brook, on the ground which once had grown the strawberries that were Mr Carey's pride and joy and which had stained his fingers and Yanina's fingers that dull red. She walked back slowly towards her house, head bent as she thought. Well this *is* going to be a fine Christmas! I can just feel it! And to cap it all there is no Benjamin. He had said without looking up from his counter and tapping the sponge more than usual: "Your bank statement is not ready. When it is I will deliver it. Would Christmas Day . . .?"

Then in the middle of these thoughts, suddenly there in front of her was this ragged person, standing quite in front of her, in her own garden; so that she could not pass!

"What do you think . . . what do you want?" Yanina said.

She said: "I came down the sidepath to see if you were here. There was no answer at the door."

"Oh Alice! Alice! Alice! Alice!"

Yanina embraced her, repeating time and time again "I didn't know it was you!"

Hesitatingly Alice went into the kitchen. "I've left my pram at the front. Is that all right?"

Seeing the concern on Yanina's face, she added "It's only pegging things and some things of mine I keep."

"I forgot," said Yanina smiling and handing Alice a cup of tea, "there's more in the pot. Is it warm enough?"

"That's good!" said Alice, "but I must get to Mr Herbert's before it begins to get dark."

"Is he expecting you?" asked Yanina.

"Not properly, no he isn't. But that's no matter." Alice paused, then asked "Does he still have spots?"

"I don't know," said Yanina, "I haven't been anywhere near there for a long time."

"I've some ointment for him. Whenever I call I bring him some and he says it does some good."

"And," said Alice giving Yanina a small bottle, "I've got some scented flower oil for you." Then she told Yanina how she had made it, and in a while they were talking of the flowers of the hedgerows, of the journeys they had made over the fields and of the chestnuts shed by the trees on the edge of the wood.

Yanina said: "Please have some goose. I was going to take the rest to Mrs Potter."

"Well, a little," said Alice.

"There's plenty of time to get to Mr Herbert's."

"We had goose when I was a girl. Its fat keeps for ever."

"Does it?" said Yanina lightly, who knew nothing of the things Alice kept in her pram.

"Well nearly ever, it does," said Alice.

As she prepared to go Yanina said: "Please Alice, as Mrs Pardoe is not at home, stay with me. You do not look well!"

"No dear, I must go to Mr Herbert's. I dare say he'll let me use his old cowshed. I'm more used to places like that, than a proper bed."

After she had gone Yanina thought, I should have asked her to call tomorrow. I'll go to Mr Herbert's in the morning and ask her. Then she rubbed a little of Alice's flower oil on her wrist. It was strong; sweet and strange as the smells of the hedgerows; like the smells on a still night in the woods; like the smells you might get lying down on a flinty field with your eyes shut, hearing the sound of a rising lark draining into a wide sky. Then she rubbed more of it on her arm and on her other arm, in almost fitful gestures, until she reeked of it.

The snow was not falling heavily. Mr Herbert was not on the telephone but Yanina reassured herself, Alice would have reached there by now!

Suddenly there was a loud knocking on her door.

Perhaps she had changed her mind!

But it was Benjamin. He stood by the door and wrinkled his nose. "I have brought your bank statement," he said, now openly sniffing; looking over Yanina's shoulder as if the source of the smell might come from the kitchen.

"What is the matter?" asked Yanina.

"The smell!" said Benjamin.

For an answer she took the bank statement from him.

"What exactly is wrong with it?" she asked.

"Oh nothing. I meant . . ."

"Goodnight," said Yanina.

"I had thought . . ." said Benjamin. "I thought that . . . oh well. Goodnight then Yanina, and a Happy Christmas!"

*   *   *

The land glistened in the fire of the dawn light. There was no breeze and the only sound was the thump of the snow as it fell off the laden branches of the hedgerow trees. Occasionally snow dislodged and sprayed as a wood pigeon flew off into the deep blue sky.

It had only snowed heavily for an hour in the afternoon of the previous day; long before Alice had left for Mr Herbert's. It had lain still and crisp all night gleaming in the harsh moonlight. It had not been a soft, motherly, hay-making sort of moon. About it were stars like the teeth of a tiger. By the morning there were tracks of all kinds. Blackbirds flew from bush to bush, startling because of their blackness and their bright yellow beaks.

Yanina looked out from the stair window. The distant hills seemed to bristle with the morning sun. She would write to Benjamin without delay! I will ask him to tea! But what if Alice couldn't come?

There was no point in asking Paul.

As Yanina set off for Mr Herbert's she thought: I hope Alice will come. I was unfriendly to Benjamin last night and this will make things all right between us again.

The lane was uphill to Mr Herbert's. Yanina undid her coat buttons. If she made sandwiches from the cold goose there would still be plenty for Mr and Mrs Potter, and there were dozens of mince pies! Suddenly she was feeling the joy of Christmas! She quickened her pace.

Since leaving the town she had noticed marks which she thought might be a fox. Quite distinctly there was the track made by Alice's pram and her footmarks preserved in yesterday's snow. There were also bird tracks and in the field by the hedges other tracks she thought must have been rabbits running about in the early morning. The fox track suddenly left the road and veered off into one of Mr Herbert's fields.

Then there were only Alice's tracks.

At last Yanina reached the gate leading to Mr Herbert's farm. She undid the last button of her coat and looked at the snow-covered town below her, saying "I must get out more often like this, or I will turn into a housebound old maid myself." As she walked the last few yards to Mr Herbert's she kicked the snow in front of her. "I even shut the door on Benjamin!"

Then she noticed something which brought her to a standstill. For a while she stared at the snow. She ran back to the gate and looked back down the lane from where she had come. There for certain were the tracks of the pram and Yanina's own tracks leading into Mr Herbert's farm. Slowly, unwillingly, she looked along the lane where it went on straight to the woods, high on the hill. Encrusted in the snow, for as far as she could see, were the tracks of Alice and her pram.

At first she seemed not to be able to reason. She called out "Alice! Alice!"

Some snow fell off a branch into the hedgerow bank.

Somewhere in the back of her mind Yanina was thinking: There is a pigeon in the bough where the snow fell. It is probably watching me.

She was calling again, cupping her hands to her mouth, "Alice! Alice!"

She turned and ran, stumbling, falling several times, to Mr Herbert's.

17

Christmas with Lord Augustus

THE ROAD PAST MR HERBERT'S gradually turned into a farm track with deep cart ruts. Alice had reached the outskirts of the wood. She had rested and looked about her. She put Mr Herbert's pot of ointment on top of her rolled up blanket, all ready. She whispered "I will go there later . . . but now!"

The snow had fallen heavily and her tracks showed clearly. Now that it had stopped there was an unearthly silence. On a rotted tree stump was an old raven, looking at Alice. It had become nearly white with snow. It was only when it shook itself and became black again that Alice noticed it. Her head throbbed as she moved towards the tree stump. She found it very difficult with the pram. It seemed as if she was saying to herself in a voice which was not her own: 'Alice! Alice, put a little goose fat on the wheels!' By the post was a peculiar haziness. Her legs, her whole body was feeling lighter.

Again: 'Alice! Goose fat!' She bent over the pram, searching. She threw out a sack of half-made pegs and a kettle. At last she found it. "Come on!" she muttered, but the rusty lid would not move. Then she gripped the lid in the folded-down pram hood, so that it was like a vice, and twisted hard with both hands.

Sometimes there was barely enough room for her between the trees. But all the time she went in a straight line, her pram gliding easily over the white ground.

She realized for certain that she was on the special path again when the rabbit sat down to watch her. She knew she had to get back to Mr Herbert's, but also she wanted to go on. Nothing could have stopped her. She waved and called out, not sure why, "Hello" and "Hello" again and a clump of snow fell from a tree as a pigeon gone to roost flew out, circling in the grey sky. It was joined by other pigeons, as it came down, gathering on the trees ahead of her. Alice went by a hollow old beech tree, and in the twig-smelling and nutshell-smelling hollow, a squirrel twitched as it lay deep in a winter's sleep.

She was passing a white slope which she recognized as the primrose bank, when she smelled a thin trace of woodsmoke. She had not stopped once, stepping lightly and swiftly with no fear of being on the wrong path. She herself was like a bird; like the birds which seemed now to have gathered to her. As a bird — going home — taken by instinct to places like India, resting their wings by the warm river banks — she was clawing her way back to the house in the woods. Like a migratory bird the pain and exhaustion had been overcome; swept aside by the long journey. Perhaps by all the journeys; the long wheeling journeys to the other villages and towns.

She was singing in her heart.

It was nearly the same as it was the first time, except that Alice was on her own with no Pig. She could smell the smoky lamp before reaching the last room. Lord Augustus was sitting at the table on which were placed two old tin mugs, a pot of tea, a bottle of wine, a bowl of cold potatoes and some gooseberry pie and custard.

"Excuse me," said Alice. "Is it all right if I bring my pram in?"

"Are you cold, Alice dear? Would you like tea to warm you up, or some wine?"

"I'm all right. I would like wine."

"Then hold the mug like this." First of all he pulled off a small piece of moss which covered a hole. Then he held the cup with one finger pressed over it.

Alice drank.

Lord Augustus said: "Happy Christmas."

Alice thought his face a trifle less hairy than it used to be but the nose was just the same as she remembered it. It was a kind looking nose; and fatty of course.

"The same to you." Then she asked by way of starting a conversation: "Do you trim your beard at all?" But she missed his answer. Instead her attention was riveted on a very strong dog kind of smell at her side.

It looked uglier than ever.

"He's waiting for a cold potato."

"Well, if you must know," said Alice, "I think it is awful to have a dog at the table. And if you don't mind my saying it, cold potatoes are boring aren't they?"

"You are absolutely right!" said Lord Augustus, "but look . . ." He went to the other end of the table and returned with a Christmas pudding, decorated with holly.

"And look at this!" He walked around the room with the lamp: the lamplight casting a curious shadow on the old plastered wall. His beard seemed to grow and twist as he moved the lamp about saying "Look Alice . . . look!"

From every available rafter and beam was hung holly and mistletoe.

From higher up, beyond the leaping shadows, Alice could hear quite distinctly the thin squeaks of bats, who, she knew, preferred to be as alone and private as the marrow in a meat bone.

Smiling, she said: "It's lovely. But in a way I wish Pig was here."

"It's different this time," said Lord Augustus.

"Then you won't go like you did?"

"I won't go," said Lord Augustus.

He rubbed his nose because of the fattiness, "There that's better," he added.

She heard the flute, at first so faintly that she could go on talking without taking too much notice. Lord Augustus was asking her if she wanted more wine.

"I cannot. It's going to my head!"

Still the notes tumbled into the room. Sometimes it seemed they came from far away, and were whisked into silence by other sounds; in the same mysterious way in which middle of the night sounds in the wood link with other sounds and are lost.

Lord Augustus was still talking. But now she could no longer hear what he was saying. She jumped on the table. The awful dog was looking not at her but at the last cold potato. She danced to the flute song around and round until in a dreamy way with bubbles of light bursting round her face she could almost see Wilfred dancing down the street twirling his hat high into the sparrowy air.

* * *

Mr Herbert was one of the search party. It did not take long.

They had followed the pram tracks to a clearing in the woods. In the clearing, poking out of the snow were some old gooseberry bushes. One or two had been trampled. One man was looking closely at the snow.

"Look at all the marks. Rabbits, birds, deer. Like a regular lot of wild things were here before us!"

One of them, Mr Herbert, paid no attention. Noticing the jar marked 'Mr Herbert' he took it and slid it into his pocket, his jaw clamped very tight, saying to himself "'Tis mine by rights!"

18

Flowers for Alice

YANINA CALLED AT THE BANK.

"Benjamin, I must speak to you. No, no: it isn't money," she said as he put his hand by the sponge. "It's about Paul. Al those flowers!"

"The town council paid for it. It came out of public funds and I'm glad," Benjamin said, "I think she deserved it."

"So do I!" she replied. "Don't you think I do? But it is no like him to do a kind thing like that; for it was Paul who pressed the council into doing it. Then there's the £5 note And that bothers me."

"What note?"

"Perhaps they mean something together. Why should he have given the newspaper man money as long as he did not report the Christmas pudding incident?"

"Yes, I heard about it."

"Well it's not in the paper. The reporter was at school with me and that's how I know."

"I don't see . . ." he began.

"Benjamin," said Yanina, "will you find out from Paul what happened? Did he say something to Alice to upset her? Will you do it for me?"

At the same time Mr and Mrs Pardoe were blaming themselves for putting dahlias out to dry and covering the picture of Wilfred and his bride and her family, all neatly gathered like starlings.

"There's no point in it, Pardoe my dear," said Mrs Pardoe. "Alice went to the woods because she wanted to and because she found what she was looking for."

"What do you mean?"

"Well we all do somehow or other I think."

"That is as maybe," said Mr Pardoe. "But I say this, I never again will hang onions from that nail."

Sooner than Benjamin expected, the following afternoon in fact, after the bank had closed, he saw Paul striding down the street.

"Hello Weekes," he said, "How's your father?"

"Very well, thank you."

"And your mother?"

"Also well. But wait if you don't mind. It was magnificent . . . the flowers, the service. And there were so many people!"

"For a childhood friend."

"But it's not like you to have done this! Is it to make you feel better for something you said or did?"

"I beg your pardon!"

"Do you feel guilty about something?"

"How dare you talk to me like this, Weekes!"

"I dare and I do," said Benjamin.

"Your bank will hear of it!"

"Oh I suppose so. Now, I have asked several people and they say Alice spoke to you before she threw the pudding. Come on! What did you say?"

Paul had turned white and was biting his lip. "Nothing! I said nothing!" he said bitterly. "Don't you see? I didn't even recognise her. I didn't know it was Alice!"

Recovering himself he added in a subdued voice, "I say Weekes, I won't mention this little argument to the bank. It won't do for us to fall out."

"Of course," said Benjamin. "Good day."

Most of the newcomers to the town disagreed with the funeral and said so in letters to the local paper. The new butcher wrote "Why should we who work hard, pay our taxes, respect the law and authority, honour such a person in this way?" And so on.

But there were almost as many people in favour as there were against. Most of those who had known Alice and who still remembered Wilfred were on the other side. This included of course Mr and Mrs Pardoe and Bony Wallis, who had disturbed those sitting next to him in the church with his distressing habit.

The preacher's wife went to the service. She was now a very old and frail lady and someone said that it did not alter the argument about Alice one way or the other because the preacher's wife was no longer quite right in the head.

So Paul simply showed once again that he was a leader: a man of action, who could alter the way things were going for him.

Because of what he did next, those who considered his judgment in the matter of the funeral expenses to be at fault now thought with everyone else that he was a Mayor to be thankful for. He said to the man who wanted to build houses in Mabbs' field: "Look, I will pay you twice the amount you paid for the field. I will on no account sell you Mabbs' yard. I will donate the whole of it to the town as a Public Park."

"You promise not to build?"

"After this conversation," said Paul truthfully, "I could not fail to keep my word."

"Then it is done!" said the other who was tired of the business anyway.

"I will erect an oak seat, with your name on it."

"It will be quite unnecessary."

"I insist," said Paul.

No one, swore Paul to himself, will know of my reasons.

Later in the week, fresh snow had fallen, and the weight of it, where the snow had blown in under the tarpaulin, had made one floor in Mabbs' building crash down upon another.

Looking at Mabbs' yard, all white and clean, Paul again thought to himself, No one will know. It will be for the 'town'. But I know that I am doing this for Alice.

No longer were there old bottles in the brook as it wound through Mabbs' field. Even the brown and black stones had been cleared away. The clumps of grass and smelly mud with insect travel-lines across them had gone. The banks had been scooped back so that the slopes were gradual. The reeds, the buttercups, the long grasses were all gone.

In place of them were scores of daffodils on either side of the brook. Parents and their children could cross in several places, using the newly-built concrete stepping stones.

The rest of the Park, including what once had been Mabbs' yard, was cut regularly with the town council lawnmower, on Tuesday afternoons or every other Tuesday afternoon, depending on the state of the grass.

One place was the same, although it was fenced off. That was the small group of pine trees. Paul had insisted that this stayed as it was. He even searched for and found the remains of the nail on which he had put the note for Alice.

In spite of his earlier intentions he quickly forgot the girl who had stood trembling under the stars defending her pig. He remembered only the messages he had left. He could even picture himself reshaping the prow of the boat before putting it in the brook water again. Then there was the pigeon Benjamin had called Mr Yates! In fact the Park which was known as Mabbs' Park had become, in Paul's mind, a monument to his own childhood.

Once or twice he had thought about Lord Augustus, but not often. When he did, it was all to do with the disturbing moment when Lord Augustus had looked at him and said quietly: "There is nothing I can tell you!"

He bought an old country house and in his garden he looked into a green-dark pond at his goldfish. He bought a pair of solid silver nutcrackers for his father's birthday.

As for Benjamin, he had looked very steadily at Paul when he called him Weekes, one day soon after he had been appointed Manager.

After that he was called Mr Weekes.

One evening, some time before the grass seed had been sown over Mabbs' yard, Benjamin had gone to the loft.

He had searched for and found the key under the tiles. Then he had looked out over the roofs and gardens.

The lawn was still there, where he had thrown a marble. But the kitchen was new and painted white and there were geraniums in baskets. He could not see the kitchen because of new lace curtains. He realized, with a stabbing pain, that he did not want to look into it anyway.

Mr Yates' box was there and three of his glass marbles. He rubbed the caked dirt off them. Then Benjamin had thumped his hands on the wall by Mr Yates' box, as if unable to contain what was in his mind one second longer than was necessary. He marched straight out without even bothering to close the loft door, straight to Yanina's house.

"I will not even bother to take a bank statement! Or the latest report on Uncle Stephen's shares! Why," he said out loud, laughing as he did so, "there has been little change in them for years!"

The brook, where it divided the back gardens was still wild and deep banked. It was like that too, on the other side of Mabbs' Park. Children still played in it and, higher up, walked through the cornfields streaked with the blood red of poppies. Some of them saw the watching eye of a raven; some fingered seeds in a seed pod, smelled the mud in the brook, as the water slid over the stones which were just like the colour of woodlice.

Some of them went to the woods on the hill.

One of these children who had Yanina's blue eyes and black hair, but who was rather shy and reserved, and was supposed to be like his father Benjamin in ways, claimed to have seen a beautiful lady called Alice in the woods, and a hairy man.

"It's what you were told!" or "You're making it up!" the others retorted.

But the boy only said:

"There were cold potatoes which she gave to a dog. She told me to guess her name. So I did. And the hairy man said: 'You're absolutely right!'"

Judith and the Traveller
Mike Scott

The bestselling first *Judith* novel. Sixteen-year-old Judith Meredith is on the run. Spider, a young traveller — one of those condemned by Irish society to live on its fringes — is also on the road. When they meet in a café, two worlds collide. The teenagers know their days together are numbered — but they are not prepared to give in without a fight.

Judith and Spider
Mike Scott

In her well-to-do world, Judith sometimes wonders whether she'll ever see Spider O'Brien again. But why does Spider wish he'd never met her?

Breaking the Circle
Desmond Kelly

When Sorcha joins an environmental group, things start to move — fast! Marches, slogans and rousing meetings follow, but the others have some dangerous ideas. Sorcha has to decide how to act. At what price does the Circle want secrecy? And is her new friend Roger all that he seems?

LAND OF DEEP SHADOW
Pat Hynes

This is the story of Packo, a hare who takes up the challenge of the Prophecy — an ancient epic tale sending him on a journey fraught with danger: preying owls, packs of squirrels and the need for wily cunning and breakneck speed to outwit and outrun the hunting hounds. But in his gruelling trek to the *Land of Deep Shadow*, Packo learns why he is not like other hares — why he alone must stand apart.

AN ECHO OF SEALS
Romie Lambkin

The summer world changes unexpectedly for Aideen and Ben. A wounded seal is rescued by the mysterious Mr Carrigan who invites the cousins to watch the night sky through his telescope. But what does he really want them to see? What is the secret of the seals?

IT'S PIN BIN DIM DOMINILLI!
Cormac MacRaois

Jim and Caitríona Doran have never seen a Dominillo until Pin appears the day before their birthday. 13 centimetres of mischief, he steals biscuits, bewilders the school bully, terrifies the local burglars, puzzles the police, and leaves the Dorans' house in an uproar. But there's more to Pin than meets the eye. His best trick is still to come ...

THE GILTSPUR TRILOGY
Cormac MacRaois

The Battle Below Giltspur, Dance of the Midnight Fire and *Lightning Over Giltspur:* Three exciting tales of adventure and mythology. 'Riveting fantasy ... a fast-moving tale where no words are wasted. From the awakening of the scarecrow Glasán, the story moves at an ever-increasing pace with strange incidents, frightening gatherings and terrifying sequences in rapid succession ... Absolutely brilliant ... exciting, funny and adventurous.'
Books Ireland.